ALL OVER THE COUNTRY, THE SHADOWS OF the approaching spaceships were engulfing the cities in darkness. It was a terrifying thing for people see. They were creeping over the United States' most beloved buildings and monuments: the Empire State Building, the George Washington Bridge, the Washington Monument, the Lincoln Memorial, the Capitol Building. The White House. The Statue of Liberty. America's symbols of liberty, freedom and peace were all being drenched in the huge, looming shadows of ships that were holding visitors from another world.

People were running in terror through their offices and down busy city streets, across grassy parks and through neighbor's yards. Panicked drivers were crashing into one another everywhere on the roads. Everyone was trying to get away from the monstrous black disks. They couldn't, though.

It was like watching flies struggling to escape from a spider when they are already caught in its web.

INDEPENDENCE DAY
———ID4———

From the screenplay and novelization by
**Dean Devlin & Roland Emmerich and
Stephen Molstad**

adapted by Dionne McNeff

HarperPrism
An Imprint of HarperPaperbacks

HarperPaperbacks *A Division of* HarperCollins*Publishers*
10 East 53rd Street, New York, N.Y. 10022

Copyright © 1996 by Twentieth Century Fox Film Corporation
All rights reserved. No part of this book may be used or reproduced in any manner whatsoever without written permission of the publisher, except in the case of brief quotations embodied in critical articles and reviews.
For information address HarperCollins*Publishers*,
10 East 53rd Street, New York, N. Y. 10022.

Cover illustration © 1996 by Twentieth Century Fox Film Corporation

First printing: July 1996

Printed in the United States of America

HarperPaperbacks and colophon are trademarks of HarperCollins*Publishers*

❖ 10 9 8 7 6 5 4

INDEPENDENCE DAY
—ID4—

THE MOON LOOKED SLIGHTLY DIFFERENT today, compared to other days. Not enough to notice, unless someone was examining it very closely through a telescope for days on end. But enough to say it was different. For one thing, it wasn't quite as bright a white. Maybe it was two shades toward gray, making its surface look like kindergarten paste instead of the usual powdery chalk. Today, something was affecting the moon's light source. There was something else, too.

A sound. Not a loud sound, but a sound no human ear could hear, not even on a place as quiet as the moon. It was more like the threat of a deep vibration that sometime soon would become a rumble.

The rumble of something so big, the moon trembled in the sky.

Too bad no one saw it coming.

THE SETI INSTITUTE WAS THE FIRST ON Earth to detect the strange change in the sky. SETI stands for the Search for Extra Terrestrial Intelligence and was a special program that was started by the government in the 1970s to look for signs of other life in the solar system. Run by some of the top scientists in the world, the SETI Institute had twelve radio telescopes spread out in a hidden valley in New Mexico. Each telescope had a dish that was over one hundred feet in diameter. They were like enormous ears pointed to the sky, trying to listen for any noise in space. These dishes were so strong, they could detect any change in the solar system's planets or nearby stars long before a regular telescope could see it.

That night a technician named Richard Yamuro was on shift. Although he was brilliant, most nights at SETI were really boring for him. Lots of information was gathered by the telescopes around the clock, but it was the computer's job to sift through it all, and this took hours and hours. There wasn't much for Richard to do, so instead he worked on his golf swing.

Richard pretended he was in the Master's Championship Golf Tournament. Golf balls were laying all over the room. He pretended to be the announcer. "Mr. Yamuro has enjoyed a great game here today, ladies and gentlemen, and now with his final hole of the day, he can seal the victory. . . ."

He positioned himself for the swing and focused his eyes on the cup in front of him where he planned to plant the ball. He sent the ball flying over the carpet, and it hit the side of the cup and rolled away. He had lost the championship.

He pretended to be the announcer again. "Oh! What an upset! Poor Mr. Yamuro—"

Just then the red emergency phone began to ring. He suddenly felt very nervous. This phone came directly from the main computer and it had never rung in the four years that Richard had worked there. When the red phone rang, it meant that the telescope dishes had discovered something out of the ordinary in space. He ran to the phone and listened to the strange noises coming from it. They were like nothing he'd ever heard before, kind of like the squeak of a balloon when the air is let out slowly. This wasn't normal space noise. This was some kind of signal. He decided to wake up the other scientists, including his boss, Dr. Nari Lang. He called him on the regular phone line.

"This better be good, Yamuro," Dr. Lang said.

"It is, sir," Richard said. "I mean, there's a disturbance, something we've never heard before coming from the main computer."

"We'll see about that," Dr. Lang said.

Dr. Lang was always in a bad mood, but especially when someone woke him up. Richard was nervous, but he knew what he heard was something out of the ordinary.

"Listen, sir." Richard held the regular phone up to the red phone, where the whining noise was still playing.

Dr. Lang wasn't angry anymore. He jumped out of bed and ran to the control room. By the time he got there, two other scientists were already busy typing into their computers. There must be a logical explanation, everyone thought. Everyone was still in their pajamas. If they hadn't been so nervous, the sight would have made them all laugh.

"What do we know so far?" asked Dr. Lang as he tied his robe.

"Well, sir," said one of the scientists, "we can confirm that the signal is unidentified."

"Hold on, now," said Dr. Lang, "let's not jump the gun."

Everyone working at SETI was always hoping for the day when the discovery of some life in outer space would be made. Flying saucers and space aliens were not just ideas from movies and books to these scientists. They were real possibilities. The only problem was that all of the scientists at SETI really wanted to discover signs of other life in the galaxy. They wanted it *too* much. They were constantly thinking they had found a sign of spaceships. It was like the little boy who cried wolf. After a while no one believed him.

It was Dr. Lang's job to check and double-check before anyone cried, "Extraterrestrials!" It wasn't hard for Dr. Lang to be the doubter in the group because he wasn't even sure if he believed in space aliens.

"It's true, sir," said Richard. "Look at this computer printout."

He handed his boss the information. Dr. Lang could not disagree.

4

"Where is the signal coming from?" Dr. Lang asked.

"This can't be right," said one of the scientists as he stared at his computer screen.

"What's wrong?" asked Dr. Lang.

"The signal is coming from roughly two hundred and forty thousand miles away," said the scientist.

"What?" everyone said together. No one could believe this was true.

"That means," Richard said very slowly, "it's coming from the moon."

Dr. Lang was always the last person to believe that someone or something else was out there, but this morning, he couldn't explain the information in front of him.

"Well, people," he said, "it looks like we might have visitors."

No one knew if they should be excited or scared.

AT THE SPACE COMMAND CONTROL Center in the Pentagon in Washington D.C., the government officials were just receiving their first message from the SETI Institute in New Mexico. The Pentagon is the largest office building in the world. All the people who were in charge of the army, navy, air force, and marines worked there. The Space Command Control Center was in charge of every space shuttle journey that astronauts made, and every satellite taking pictures in space, so that the government could learn more about the solar system. It was a very busy place full of the United States' top space specialists.

Even though it was two hours before sunrise, people were already busy at work. When the message had come from SETI, the head officer at Space Command decided he had to wake up his boss, General Grey.

General Grey was the chairman of the Joint Chiefs of Staff and one of the president of the United States' closest advisors and friends. He was about sixty years old and smart as a whip. Everyone was slightly afraid of General Grey, and he knew it. He knew that Space Command wouldn't dare wake him up and ask him to come into work at four a.m. unless it was really important. And it was.

As General Grey pulled into the parking lot, he was met by Space Command's first in command, a bright young man who at this very moment looked very nervous and scared. He saluted the general as he got out of his car.

"Who else knows about this?" was the first thing General Grey barked at the young man. This was no time for the usual "good mornings."

"SETI in New Mexico, sir." The young soldier had to run to keep up with General Grey, who didn't wait for an answer to his question. By now, Grey was already in the door of the Pentagon and half-way down the main hallway. The young man caught up to him just in time to run his identification card through the lock, so the security doors to the Space Command Center would slide open for the General.

The Command Center looked a lot like the SETI Institute, only multiplied by ten. A dozen technicians sat at their desks and busily typed away at two dozen computers. No one was in their pajamas here, but everyone looked like they could use some sleep. General Grey and the commanding officer walked across the busy room.

"Something is jamming satellites all over the world, sir, including our own," said the commanding officer. "Take a look at these monitors."

The commanding officer pointed to a row of television monitors tuned into news broadcasts from all over the world. Every few seconds, the picture in each monitor looked fuzzy and rolled up and down. These channels usually came in crisp and clear, but today the monitors looked like they were stuck between two stations and needed a quick trip to the repair shop.

"What is the press saying?" asked General Grey.

"Nothing yet, sir. They've agreed to hold off and wait for more tests to be run," said the commanding officer.

General Grey was losing patience. He was used to plans and information, not mysteries.

"So," General Grey squinted at the officer, "what is it?"

"Well, sir." The commanding officer was sweating. "I'm sorry to say we don't know, but before the satellites jammed, we did get these."

The commanding officer walked to a large, brightly lit table and set a few blurry photographs on top of it. The photographs showed a grainy shape that didn't look like anything any of the officers had ever seen before. It wasn't a star, and it wasn't a planet. It was very large and shaped sort of like a helmet. Everyone just stared at the photos. They thought if they looked long enough, they could figure out what it was. General Grey couldn't take the suspense any longer.

"Is it a meteor?" asked General Grey.

"No, sir, definitely not," said the commanding officer.

"How do you know?" asked General Grey.

"Well, uh . . ." The commanding officer knew that General Grey was about to flip his lid. "Because it's slowing down," he said.

"It's *what*?" screamed the general.

"It's slowing down, sir . . . General . . . sir," said the commanding officer. His voice almost cracked he was so nervous.

The only possible explanation for an unidentified flying object would be a meteor or a comet, but there was no way either would ever slow down. Now General Grey was as confused as everyone else, and when General Grey got confused he got really, really mad. He walked over to a phone and picked it up.

"Get me the secretary of defense," he said.

After a pause, the Pentagon operator came back on the line. "I'm sorry, sir, but his wife says he's sleeping," she said.

"Then wake him up!" General Grey yelled.

AT THE WHITE HOUSE, PRESIDENT Thomas J. Whitmore was sitting in bed reading a stack of papers when the phone rang.

"Hi, it's me," said a friendly voice. The voice belonged to Marilyn Whitmore, the First Lady of the United States and loving wife of the president.

President Whitmore smiled and stretched a little. "Hi honey, what time is it there?"

Mrs. Whitmore was in Los Angeles for a charity event. "It's two in the morning," she said. "Don't tell me I woke you?"

"As a matter of fact you did, dear," said the president. Marilyn was always getting after him to get more rest, but since he had become president, it never seemed like there were enough hours in the day.

Marilyn smiled. "Liar," she said.

Lying beside President Whitmore, fast asleep, was his six-year-old daughter, Patricia. She could tell by the way her daddy was talking that Mommy was on the phone. She awoke instantly, holding out her hands for the phone. "Please can I talk to Mommy?"

"Hold on a second, sweetheart," President Whitmore said to Patricia.

"The munchkin is awake," he told his wife. "Let me put her on."

"You didn't let her stay up all night watching TV, did you?" asked Marilyn.

"Of course not," he said. But he had. The president could be tough with top leaders all over the world, but he could not refuse a thing to his beautiful little daughter, who was now begging to speak to her mom.

"You're flying back after the luncheon, right?" asked the president.

"Yes, I'll see you soon," said Marilyn.

The president handed the phone to his grateful daughter. He got out of bed and turned on the television. The TV picture was fuzzy and rolling just like the ones at the Pentagon Space Command Center. He paused a moment to listen to one of those talk shows where a bunch of serious-looking people sat in a circle and talked about whether or not he was doing a good job as president. They always said he wasn't.

"Look, just because he was a heroic pilot in the Gulf War doesn't mean he would have any clue how to run the country," one of the serious men said to the others. "It's the country's fault for electing him in the first place."

"Ha!" President Whitmore laughed. "That's a good one!" These TV discussion groups never had anything good to say about him, so he just tried to keep a good sense of humor about it.

Whitmore was very young to be the president. He

still had his boyish good looks, and he was very charming and likable. He had won the office by promising change and cutting through all of the Washington politics. Although he had been able to make some things better, it hadn't been enough for most people. Right now Whitmore wasn't very popular with the public, but he believed he could change that, too, through more hard work to improve the country.

After saying goodnight to her mother and hanging up the phone, Patricia grabbed the remote control from her dad's hand and began flipping channels until she found cartoons. The picture was still fuzzy and rolling.

"Honey, it's too early for cartoons. You should go back to sleep for a little while," said the president as he headed to the other room to put on his robe and slippers.

"I know, but sometimes the TV helps me sleep," said Patricia. "Why is the picture all messed up?"

"This is what the TV looks like when it's too early for little girls to be watching it." He rushed back into the room and tickled her.

"Oh, Daddy," she said through her giggles, "that's ridiculous."

"Ridiculous, huh? Good word, I like that," he said. Patricia wasn't going to win him completely over, though. He walked over to the TV and turned it off. "Now, get some sleep." He headed out the door to the breakfast room.

TWO SERVANTS WERE BUSY PREPARING breakfast for the president's communications director, Constance Spano, when he walked in. She was already dressed for the day in a pale peach suit and poring over a stack of newspapers in front of her on the table. She didn't look happy.

"You're up early this morning, Connie," said the president cheerily.

"I can't believe what these pigs are saying!" she said without looking up from the papers.

"*Good morning,* Connie," he tried again.

"Hmm?" she looked up at him. "Oh, sorry, good morning," she said.

Constance Spano, or Connie as everyone called her, had been with the president for many years. When he was a senator and had decided to run for the office, she was in charge of his campaign.

Now that Whitmore was president, it was Connie's job to make sure that his activities were being covered by the newspapers and TV. Wherever he went, whomever he met, whatever bills he was trying to pass or speeches he was making, Connie was there for him. She was loyal to her boss and very dedicated to her job. Whenever a press conference was held, she was the one who had to answer all of the tough questions that the journalists shouted. In the beginning, her job had been quite easy because the president was so well liked, but now every day was a battle.

"Have you seen *The Post* this morning? Can you believe what they're saying?" she asked.

The president smiled. "You should have heard what they were saying about me on the TV this morning. You would have had a fit."

"I'm having a fit already, can't you tell?" she asked. Sometimes Connie was frustrated by the president's easy-going nature. He never allowed criticism of his performance to bother him. He let Connie get upset for him. He knew that by the end of the day she would have struck back at anyone who attacked him.

"Every day lately, it's the same thing," she said. "They keep attacking you for being too young. They say you don't know what you're doing."

The president was eating his breakfast and hardly seemed to be paying attention to what Connie was saying. She continued on. There was something more she really wanted to say.

"America is listening to the press, Tom. They think you've given up." Connie realized that she had probably gone too far, but she felt like he had to hear it. Lately, she had been disappointed in the way he was handling things, too.

President Whitmore looked up from his coffee and Danish. Now, she had his attention. He knew she was only speaking to him with such brutal honesty because she was a good friend and she respected him very much. Whitmore knew it might have looked to some like he had given up lately, but he hadn't. He thought it was better to get a lot of little things accomplished than spend all his time and energy on the big problems. Accomplishing the little problems would chip away at the big ones, he thought. It would take time for the Americans, and Connie, to understand his new approach.

Connie tried to lighten the mood. "Well, there is some good news," she said. "*The Observer* has voted you one of the ten best-looking men in America!"

Whitmore laughed and wiggled his eyebrows up and down. "Now, we're getting somewhere."

Just then, they were interrupted by a young man who appeared in the doorway.

"Excuse me, Mr. President," he said. "The secretary of defense is on the phone for you. I'm sorry to interrupt, sir, but he said it was an emergency."

"Okay." The president wiped his mouth with his napkin and walked over to the breakfast room phone. "Let's start our day," he said to Connie as he picked up the phone.

"Yes, what is it?" asked the president into the receiver.

For the next two minutes he listened and the pleasant smile that had been on his face two minutes ago vanished completely. Connie could tell that the emergency was serious. She tried to imagine what it could possibly be.

IT WAS A BEAUTIFUL, SUNNY DAY IN NEW
York City. The kind of day that only happens in
picture postcards. At Cliffside Park in New Jersey, a
group of elderly men had gathered as they did every
morning for a game of chess. Today they had a
beautiful view of Manhattan across the Hudson River.
Of course, no one much noticed, though. They were
too busy chatting, arguing, and gossiping about their
families, their neighbors, politicians, TV programs—
just about anything anyone could think of. In the
middle of all this, the chess games went on.

David Levinson was the youngest of the chess
challengers at thirty-eight years old. Three mornings a
week he would meet his father, Julius, for a game in
the park before he went to work. David stood out
among the aging crowd: he was tall and thin and had
all of his hair. Any one of these features would have
set him apart, but all three together made him
positively shocking. He and Julius were also the best
chess players in the park on any given day, so when
they began their game, everyone quietly noticed.
Julius sat hunched over, chomping on his cigar as he
waited for his son to make his next move.

"What are you waiting for? Move! Move!" said
Julius.

"I'm thinking," said David.

"So think already," Julius huffed. Everyone in the

park enjoyed the father and son's comical way of talking to one another even more than they enjoyed watching them play.

Finally, David made his move. With lightning speed, Julius took his turn. David looked up at his father with a curious sort of grin on his face. He then looked back down to the board for another planning session.

"Again! He's thinking!" Julius announced to the park.

Julius reached into his crumpled paper bag to lift out his coffee and started to fiddle with the lid. This got David's attention.

"Hey, Dad," said David, "where's the mug I bought you?"

"It's in the sink, dirty from the day before yesterday," said Julius.

"Do you have any idea how long it takes for one of those cups to decompose?" David was very active in a number of environmental groups. One of the groups was specifically dedicated to banning the use of Styrofoam cups in the fast food industry. Now his own father sat before him with one in his hand.

Julius always had a snappy comeback for his son. "If you don't move soon, I'll start to decompose."

David grumbled and made his move. Julius moved his piece without a moment's hesitation. It was David's turn again. Julius continued to fiddle with his cup and could see the aggravation in his son's face. He decided to try and change the subject. But of course, as fathers often do, he only changed the subject to something equally irritating.

"So, David," said Julius, "I've been meaning to talk to you . . . "

David glanced up at his father with a look that said, "Don't start, Dad," but it was way too late. Julius was on a roll.

"It's nice that you've been spending all of this time with me, but it's been what? Four years?" asked Julius.

"Three years," David corrected.

"Three years, four years. David, you're still wearing your wedding ring. It's time to move on! This isn't healthy!" said Julius. Now he had the attention of the entire park. Everyone knew the sad story of David's wife leaving him.

David was embarrassed. He looked around at the interested audience and tried to switch the subject.

"Healthy! Pops, look who's talking healthy," said David as he pointed to the cigar that Julius had been chewing on for the last hour. "Smoking," said David, "is not healthy. Now come on, let's play the game."

Suddenly, David's pager started to beep. He always brought his pager with him in case his office needed to reach him, but he hardly ever paid any attention to it.

"How many times is that now?" asked Julius. "Are you trying to get fired?"

David grabbed his pager off the table, moved his

queen, rose up from the table, kissed his dad on the cheek, and said, "Checkmate. See you tomorrow, Dad." He grabbed his bicycle and left Julius in a rare state of speechlessness. What just happened? Julius wondered.

"Wait a minute, wait a minute," hollered Julius, "that's not checkmate!" He shook his finger in the air to the crowd who were beginning to pack up their things. "That's not checkmate!" He looked down at the board again and realized that it was, indeed, checkmate. He had lost to David, once again. He held his chin in his hands like a frustrated child and yelled to the long-gone David, "You know you could let an old man win once in a while! It wouldn't kill ya." Secretly though, Julius was proud to have the smartest person in the park for a son.

DAVID WEAVED HIS BICYCLE THROUGH THE bumper to bumper traffic that was slowly edging its way across the George Washington Bridge and into downtown Manhattan. On most days, David could tune out all of the racket around him. The blaring radios, honking horns, and screaming people would all fade away, but today, everyone seemed even more agitated than usual. *I wonder what's going on?* David thought. *Maybe it's a full moon.* He knew that if the outside world was feeling a little crazier than usual, that could only mean that the people inside the offices of

Compact Cable Corporation where he worked were really bad off. This was due to his boss, Marty Gilbert, the most nervous man alive. There was no doubt that Marty would have the whole office whipped into a frenzy if he was having a bad day. David even felt a little bit guilty for not answering Marty's many pages as he waltzed into work with his bike slung over his shoulder. He realized that everyone was busy bustling about. Marty rushed up to David the second he saw him.

"David, David," said Marty, "why don't you ever answer my pages?" Marty was about to rip his own hair out.

"I was ignoring you." David smiled. "So what's the big emergency?"

Marty started talking a mile a minute. "It started this morning," he said. "Every channel is full of fuzz and distortion. The picture won't stop rolling. No one knows what's going on. We've got to do something. Customers are frantic. The phones are ringing off the hook."

David parked his bike against the soda machines in the middle of the office. David wasn't upset, or even worried. In fact, he was sort of intrigued. Today, unlike most days, would be a challenge for him. David loved puzzles, and this sounded like a good one. Marty didn't know how to get his genius staff member to see the urgency in the situation and get a move on. He looked like he might cry. He quickly chugged the last of his diet soda and tossed it in the regular trash can that sat next to the "Recycle" bin. This set David off. The cable problems would have to wait.

"Marty, my God, there's a reason we have bins labeled 'recycle.'" He rummaged through the trash and pulled out three more cans. He stared at Marty accusingly.

"What is this?" asked David.

"So sue me! David, this is serious, please!"

David replaced the cans in the correct bin and shook his head in frustration. *What would it take to teach the world to conserve and recycle? We're killing our beautiful planet,* David thought, *and no one cares.*

Marty couldn't take the delay. He began to push David into his office, forcing him to refocus his attention on the problem at hand.

David looked at the information sitting on his desk and looked across the room at the wall of TV monitors which showed that the fuzzy, rolling picture was affecting every channel. David's mind began to tick.

"Did you try to switch the transponder channels?" asked David. This was the first thing to try if a channel's picture went bad. Marty was no technical wizard, but even he knew this was the first thing to do to adjust the picture.

"Please, would I be this panicked if it was something that simple?" asked Marty.

David examined the computer readouts. He was also puzzled.

"Marty, you had better switch to another satellite while I work on this."

Again, Marty was frustrated by David's simple suggestions. "I wish I could," he said. "Every communications satellite is experiencing the same distortion, or else they are gone completely." It was like saying every car in America had broken down at the same moment, and no one could drive. David wrinkled his brow.

"That's impossible," said David. Now he was really intrigued.

All Marty could do was shrug his shoulders. As David pored over the computer readouts again, Marty rushed out of the room to go worry somewhere else.

SMACK!

A small hand slammed down on the top of an old television set. This woke up Miguel, who was trying to sleep in the back of the motor home. He rubbed his eyes to see what the noise was and—*smack!*—it happened again. It was his little brother Troy sitting in the front of the motor home trying to get the TV's fuzzy, rolling picture to tune in.

"Stop it, Troy!" yelled Miguel.

"It's all fuzzy!" Troy yelled back.

"You're going to break it. Just leave it alone," said Miguel.

He knew there was no sleeping now, so he got up

and walked to the front of the motor home. He was still dressed in his blue jeans from the night before. He sat down next to Troy in the cramped little table booth and saw that the TV was really messed up. He looked out the window and saw a bunch of kids who lived in the other motor homes playing games in the dirt. They were about forty miles outside of Los Angeles, but it felt like two million. It was a depressing place to live. Miguel and Troy had lived there with their sister Alicia and father Russell for over a year. Some days were a lot worse than others.

Two weeks ago, Miguel had graduated from high school, but he didn't go to the ceremony because he was afraid that his father would show up. Russell could be very embarrassing, especially if he was drunk, and he usually was. Ever since their mom had died, things had gone from bad to worse. At seventeen, Miguel had to support the whole family with whatever kind of work he could find. He got up from the table to make Troy some breakfast. He handed Troy a small brown bottle.

"Here, take your medicine," said Miguel.

"I don't need it," said Troy as he pushed the bottle away.

"Just take it butt-munch," said Miguel.

Every day there was a battle over Troy taking his medicine. He had a problem with his adrenal cortex and had to take medicine for it every day or he could get very sick, even die. It's how his mom had died.

Troy continued to whack the side of the TV and ignore Miguel.

"Listen Mr. Kung Fu Television Repair Man, I told you. It's not the set. It's the whatever—" Miguel waved his hands in the air "—the airwaves, so leave it alone."

Just then, Alicia threw open the little screen door and hopped in the motor home. Her Walkman was so loud, her music filled the whole motor home. Her clothes were too short and too tight, and for a fourteen-year-old, she was wearing way too much makeup. All she could think about was some older boy falling in love with her and taking her away from this lousy motor home park and her boring family. Every time Miguel looked at her, he just got frustrated. All she cared about was herself, he thought. He threw a dish towel at her and it landed right in her face.

"Hey!" she shrieked. "What was that for?"

"You're supposed to make sure Troy takes his medicine, Alicia. That's your only job and you never do it!" said Miguel.

"You make sure," said Alicia. "I'm too busy."

"Too busy doing what? Scrounging around for some guy—" Miguel couldn't finish because a red Chevy truck had just screeched to a stop outside of their motor home. The driver sat in the cab for a moment. He looked like he was trying to cool down. When he got out, though, it didn't look like it had done much good. He pounded on the motor home door. Miguel knew this could only mean one thing. His father had screwed up, again.

"Good morning, Lucas," said Miguel. He was trying to pretend that this was a friendly visit, but he knew it wasn't. Lucas owned a nearby farm and Russell had been hired three days ago to spray it for insects. It was the first job Russell had been offered in six months. Lucas held up a handful of rotten vegetables.

"Look at this! Do you like these? Thanks to your father, I've got a whole crop that looks like this! Where is he?"

Miguel tried to cover for his dad. He had no idea where he was. Probably in the bar down the street.

"Uh . . ." said Miguel, "I think he said he had to refuel this morning. There must have been some kind of problem."

"We both know what the problem is, Miguel," said Lucas. Everyone knew Russell was a drunk. Lucas had just tried to give him some work because he felt sorry for the kids.

Troy continued to smack the side of the TV. This really set Miguel on edge.

"Troy, stop it! I swear to God!" said Miguel through his teeth. He tried to smile at Lucas. He felt like his world was falling apart.

Lucas softened his voice. He really did feel sorry for Miguel.

"Look Miguel," said Lucas, "I'm sorry, but if he's

not in the air in twenty minutes, I'm going to have to get someone else."

Lucas began to walk back to his pickup. Miguel yelled after him.

"Twenty minutes! He'll be there!"

Alicia nudged her way under her brother's arm to wave good-bye to the handsome man with the car and the farm.

"Bye, Lucas," said Alicia. She smiled sweetly.

Troy made fun of his sister for her shameless flirting.

"Geez, Alicia, get a life!"

"Shut up, Troy." She ran to the back of the motor home to sulk.

Now Miguel had to find Russell and quick. He ran outside and hopped on his beat-up motorcycle. He stared at the handle bars and said to himself, "Russell, where the heck are you?"

AT THE SPACE COMMAND CENTER IN THE Pentagon, they were receiving some more detailed photographs and information about the large helmet-shaped object in the sky. They had learned that it was hiding itself behind the moon. When the moon moved, the ship moved. Space Command had to reposition their satellites so they could get a good look at the thing. Cameras were beaming pictures back down to earth, and what Space Command saw they didn't like.

The bottom of the object was breaking apart into dozens of round pieces, but even the pieces were huge. They were spinning around and out of enormous openings in the bottom of the ship. It looked like dozens of screws untwisting themselves and falling out of their holes. Space Command couldn't believe what they were seeing. Everyone's eyes were glued to the screen. The large disks were headed this way. . . . They were falling toward earth.

BACK AT THE WHITE HOUSE, PEOPLE were bustling about everywhere. Connie had been sitting in her office, talking on the phone. She was trying to convince her contacts at all of the news stations to not say anything on the news that might cause people to panic. It was a hard thing to say because she was feeling pretty panicked herself.

The problem was, everyone who could get through was calling the White House to get an answer. How was it possible that every TV in North America, Europe, and Asia could be screwed up at the same time unless something was wrong in space? Some reporters were saying it was because of some kind of nuclear testing experiments. Connie didn't know anything more than anyone else did, but it was her job to try to keep people calm until they did know. At this very moment, it was a pretty tough job.

In the Oval Office, where the president held his

most private and important meetings, President Whitmore sat around a table with his top advisors, including his chief of staff, his Secretary of Defense Albert Nimziki, and General Grey. None of them had seen the latest pictures of the huge disks falling out of the bottom of the giant thing that was hiding behind the moon. At this time, General Grey was trying to make everyone feel better about the situation.

"I want to remind everyone," said General Grey, "that our satellites are not reliable at the moment. It isn't clear whether this thing will be able to get any closer to us, or whether it wants to."

As the Secretary of Defense, Nimziki always assumed the worst possible situation and then planned from there. He didn't think it was right to hope that the massive space object wouldn't get any closer. He thought they should expect it to get very close very soon.

"So what if it does get closer?" Nimziki asked. "I think we'd better point some missiles at it and get ready to blow it out of the sky."

Most people in the room disliked Secretary Nimziki. He was smart, but he only cared about himself. Whenever he made a suggestion, everyone assumed he would benefit from it. General Grey disliked him more than anyone he'd ever met. President Whitmore was such a level-headed man, General Grey couldn't understand why he kept someone like Secretary Nimziki around.

"Forgive me, Secretary Nimziki," said General Grey, "but that absolutely seems like the wrong thing to do. What if our missiles miss?"

General Grey had seen the first photos that had come in and had studied more of the information that the satellites had gathered than the other people in the room. Although he hadn't said the word out loud yet, General Grey now believed that the object hiding behind the moon was a spaceship. He was concerned that if they shot missiles at the craft and missed, they could make whoever was inside very angry.

Secretary Nimziki spoke to General Grey in a very loud voice to make sure everyone could hear him.

"It's time for you to upgrade the situation to a 'yellow alert,'" he said. This would mean calling every member of the military back to their bases on the Fourth of July holiday weekend. This would definitely scare everyone in America and that was something they really didn't want to do. Nimziki's suggestion silenced the room.

Before General Grey could respond, the door opened and in walked the commanding officer from the Space Command Center at the Pentagon. He still looked scared. He cleared his throat before speaking to General Grey. The rest of the room listened closely.

"Excuse me, sir, I have some updated information to give you," he said.

"Yes, go ahead," said General Grey.

"The object has settled into a stationary orbit. It's moving with the moon to keep itself behind it."

"That's good news," General Grey said.

"Well," the commanding officer's voice started to crack again, "not really, sir. The object established its orbit at 10:53 A.M. local time and at 11:01 A.M., about thirty-six pieces of the object began to separate off the main body."

"Pieces?" asked President Whitmore.

"Yes, sir," said the officer, "large round disks, sir. We estimate that each disk is approximately fifteen miles in diameter." He laid the latest photos in front of the president.

The president then asked the question that everyone in the room was afraid to say. "Are they headed toward earth?"

The commanding officer gulped hard. Everyone heard it. "Yes, sir. At Space Command, we estimate that the disks will be entering our atmosphere in the next twenty-five minutes."

At that moment, everyone's worst nightmare seemed to be coming true. The earth was being visited—maybe even invaded—by something from another world, and there was hardly any time to do anything. Secretary Nimziki broke the silence.

"Mr. President, given this new information, whether we like it or not, we must go to a 'yellow alert.' Our military must be ready for whatever may happen."

No one in the room could disagree.

BEEP, BEEP, BEEP. A YELLOW LIGHT WAS blinking and beeping. David opened the microwave door and grabbed his thawed lunch. He sat in his chair with his long legs folded under him and one arm wrapped around his head. He always twisted his body into strange positions when he was thinking really hard. At his desk, he continued to pore over all of the information. His office was jammed full of computer equipment and plants. His portable laptop computer was running through more numbers on his desk. The same group of numbers repeated themselves every twenty seconds. Marty burst into his office and ruined his concentration.

"Please tell me you're getting somewhere," said Marty.

"I think I've figured this out, but I can't figure it out," said David as he picked at his lunch.

"What?" asked Marty.

"Hmm?" David looked up. He didn't realize he hadn't made any sense. "Well, what I mean is, I know what the problem is, I just can't understand why it's happening."

Marty didn't care why the problem was occurring, he just wanted it fixed.

"So? So, when can you fix it by?" Marty asked.

David was still fascinated by the problem itself. He began to explain it to Marty. "There's a weird signal that isn't ours inside our own signal on the satellite feed. I have absolutely no idea where it's coming from, but I've never seen anything like it. Somehow the weird signal got inside every signal in the sky. That's why every TV is messed up right now."

Marty hadn't understood a word David had just said. He asked his question again. "So? So, when can you fix it by?"

David was proud of himself for figuring out the signal within a signal, but he knew it was time to make Marty happy, too. "I'm going to block it out. It won't take long, maybe a couple of hours."

Marty started to do a little happy dance in David's office. He almost knocked over a plant. "So we'll be the only guys in town with a clear picture? Oh, David, I love you!" Then Marty danced right out of David's office.

"Whoa, Marty," David said, smiling, "you're welcome."

David went back to work.

MIGUEL HAD BEEN ALL OVER THE VALLEY looking for his father, Russell. He was running out of ideas and running out of gas. Just then, he saw him. Russell's old red biplane was dipping up and down over someone's tomato field. All Miguel knew was that the field didn't belong to Lucas, the man who had hired his crazy dad.

Russell saw his son on the ground waving him down. He stupidly waved back and yelled to him.

"Hey, Miguel, how are ya?" He was paying no attention to the trees right in front of him. When he turned back around, he had to quickly tilt the plane sideways so he wouldn't crash. He made another lazy circle over the field as he laughed and hollered. Russell was proud of himself for being such a good pilot.

Miguel watched him bring the plane in for a landing and wanted to cry, but he couldn't. Not in front of anybody else.

The plane coughed and sputtered to a stop. It looked like Snoopy's plane when he pretended to be the Red Baron—like a cartoon plane that wouldn't really fly. Miguel skidded to a halt next to him.

"Did you see that, Miguel?" asked Russell. "Boy, that was some flying, I'll tell you. I still got it." He stood up in the cockpit and whacked himself in his big belly. He tried to get out of the plane, but practically fell over the side. He was drunk again.

"What do you think you're doing, Russell?" Miguel asked.

"What does it look like I'm doing?" he asked. "I'm puttin' food on the table for my kids. That's what."

"It's the wrong field. Lucas' farm is on the other side of town," Miguel said. He could hardly look at Russell. Under his breath he added, "Idiot."

Russell was genuinely confused by this new

information. He could have sworn he was in the right place, but he was used to being wrong.

"Are you sure?" Russell asked.

"Don't you know that Lucas was doing you a favor? Everyone in town thinks you're completely crazy. What are we supposed to do now, huh? Where are we going to go now?"

Miguel's eyes were hot with angry tears. He didn't know what to do. Ever since his mother had died, he had been trying to hold this family together. But the man he was looking at right now, who was so drunk and crazy that he didn't even know where he was at eleven in the morning, was not worth keeping around anymore. He wasn't even Miguel's father by blood, just his stepfather. It was time to get away from him, thought Miguel. He peeled out on his motorcycle, making plans for the future as he drove away.

Of course, Miguel didn't know that a fifteen-mile-wide disk from another world was headed their way. Miguel's plans would be changing.

IN THE MIDDLE OF THE DESERT IN Northern Iraq, in the Middle East, refugees slept in their flimsy tents. They were enjoying their last hour of sleep, not knowing that they would soon wake up to find a mysterious disk-shaped object hidden in a cloud of fire coming toward them in the sky.

When the first man came out of his tent and began

to prepare his morning coffee, he turned to see why the sky was so warm and bright so early in the morning. He stood frozen and speechless. It looked as if a giant piece of the sky was on fire. The fireball was the size of a mountain range. It was bright orange in the middle, and gray and white on the edges, and it was rolling toward them like a storm cloud ready to burst.

In minutes, the entire camp was awake, running and screaming. They were trying desperately to escape whatever was heading their way. But whatever it was, it had no plans of stopping. This was the first sighting of the massive disks as they entered the earth's atmosphere.

ON A SUBMARINE IN THE PACIFIC OCEAN the second disk was spotted entering the atmosphere. All of the radar and infrared monitors became completely blank as the massive disk filled the sky above them. The sailors on board began to panic. The submarine's commander shouted orders to his crew and reported the blackout to headquarters in Washington, D.C. The message was then quickly relayed to the White House.

The commanding officer from the Space Command Center updated everyone on the situation. "We have two confirmed visual contacts. One over Iraq and one over the Pacific Ocean."

"Where in the Pacific?" asked Secretary Nimziki.

General Grey entered the room with a stack of paper in his hand and more news. "Mr. President, they've just spotted another one off the California coastline."

The tension in the room was growing by the minute. The military had been called back to their bases on "yellow alert," and a fleet of nuclear submarines was ready to launch with a moment's notice. Battleships had also been deployed on both coasts, and President Whitmore had ordered that a military plane be sent up for a close inspection of one of the large disks. In spite of all of this instant preparation, everyone still felt helpless. Who knew what to expect in the next few hours, even days? They were the ones in charge of protecting the country, and they had no idea what else they could do but wait and see what was going to happen next.

Connie rushed into the room and whispered to the president, who then walked over to the TV and flipped it on. The reception was still rolling and fuzzy, but on the screen they could see a ball of fire in the sky like the one that had appeared a few hours earlier in Iraq. It was rolling over the city of Novomoskovsk in Russia. It was only 6:30 in the morning, but people were running and screaming everywhere. The reporter who was covering the event was almost knocked over several times. No one could take their eyes off of the strange boiling ball. Whatever it was, it didn't look friendly.

General Grey was on the phone again, and he

signaled to the president. "Mr. President, we have the military plane that is headed toward the West Coast on the line. They will be arriving in three minutes."

"Put them on the speakerphone," said the president.

The room full of worried people gathered around the phone. Many of them were saying a silent prayer for the men about to check out the huge disks first-hand. Even though the plane was three thousand miles away, the pilot's report was coming in loud and clear.

"Negative, we have zero visibility," said the pilot. He repeated, "We can't see a thing up here."

The inside of the aircraft was packed with wall-to-wall computers and radar equipment. It was the best equipment the country had to offer, and it was all malfunctioning.

"We can't get any kind of read-out on what's in front of us," the pilot said.

There was a moment of tense silence, and then the pilot came back on the line. "Wait a minute," he said, "it may be clearing. It looks a little better ahead."

Seconds passed. Everyone was at the edge of their seat. Then they heard it. The pilot's last words.

"Jesus God! The sky's on fire!" They could hear glass shatter and the pilot's screams. The plane plowed into a solid wall of flame five miles high and twenty miles long. The phone line went dead.

"Get them back on the line!" General Grey snapped to one of his men.

"The line's gone, sir," the man said.

Another military officer stepped into the room to bring more bad news. He addressed President Whitmore, but he had everyone's attention. "Excuse me, Mr. President, two more disks have been spotted over the Atlantic. One is moving toward New York and the other is headed in this direction."

"How much time do we have?" the president asked.

"Less than ten minutes."

Secretary Nimziki tried to quickly take control of the situation. He addressed the entire room. "Prepare Air Force One. We must take the president to a secure location immediately."

People began to bustle about. Everyone except the president. "I'm not leaving," he said.

Nimziki was stunned and so was the rest of the room.

"That is not a wise move, Mr. President," Nimziki said.

The president glared at him and issued a set of commands. "I want the vice president, the cabinet, and the joint chiefs taken to a secured location. I'm staying at the White House."

"But, Mr. President—" Secretary Nimziki interrupted.

"I'm not going to add to the panic that people will be feeling in the next few minutes as they see these disks getting close to their homes. Besides, so far these things haven't become hostile. For the moment, let's assume they won't." He walked over to Connie. "Connie, let's issue statements on the news telling people to stay indoors and not panic. Tell them I will address the nation shortly."

"Yes, sir." Connie had already planned a statement.

The meeting broke up immediately and people rushed about in every direction. The president walked over to his desk to collect his things. General Grey approached him.

"With your permission, Mr. President, I'd like to remain at your side," he said.

President Whitmore looked up and gave his old friend a grateful smile. "I had a feeling you would."

Secretary Nimziki overheard the conversation, and didn't want to be left out.

"Then I'll stay, too," Nimziki said.

"Great," said the president. He'd had enough of Nimziki for awhile, but if he insisted on staying, he could stay. Nimziki walked away from the two men, obviously pleased with himself.

"Mr. President . . ." General Grey hesitated. This question was tough. "What if they do become hostile?"

President Whitmore didn't know what to say. "Then God help us."

EVERYONE AT COMPACT CABLE WAS GLUED to the TV. News reports were coming in from all over that showed the fiery balls in the sky moving toward the world's largest cities. No one knew what to make of it. Most people still wanted to believe that it had something to do with the weather. Maybe David was right, some of them thought, *maybe we did ruin the planet. Maybe the hole in the ozone layer has become too big and this is what it looks like.* Everyone was trying desperately to think of some logical reason for what they were seeing in the sky. Everyone except David, that is. He was so busy checking his discovery of the signal inside a signal that he hadn't even noticed what was going on.

David walked up to a group of his coworkers who were all silently watching the TV. The picture was still a mess. Marty sat in the front with his jaw wide open.

"Marty, great news, I know how to filter this signal inside our signal," said David.

"Huh, what?" Marty had long forgotten about his cable problems. He was beginning to jump to his own conclusions about what this strange thing in the sky could be. He looked up at David and realized that his employee had no idea what was going on. "David, aren't you watching this? It's horrible!"

"Watching what?" David turned to look at the TV and saw the president of the United States' communications director, Constance Spano, addressing the press and the nation. She was asking that everyone try to remain calm and stay indoors if possible. Seeing Connie shot a pang of sadness through David. Connie was still David's wife, but they had split up three years ago. He hadn't seen her in months. She still looked beautiful to him, but very far away. He tried to listen to what she was saying.

"Three different objects are about to appear over American cities. One is off the coast of Los Angeles, and the other two are headed for New York and Washington, D.C.," Connie announced.

David felt a chill travel through the room. One of his coworkers spoke up.

"Maybe it's debris from an asteroid."

"Oh, pul-leeze," said Marty in his exaggerated way, "look, they're not falling, they're flying! Get it? They're flying across the sky toward our major cities. They're flying saucers invading earth!" Marty was not handling the situation very well, but nobody really knew what they should do.

"This building has an old bomb shelter. Let's head down there now," someone finally said.

Marty looked to David for comfort. He was beside himself. "I'd better call my mother!" He ran off, biting his nails.

David stood there in a state of shocked amazement. He looked at the information about the satellite disturbance that he held in his hand and then stared again at the pictures of the fiery ball on TV. Then something clicked. He knew the two things were related.

"My God!" he said to himself. "The signal!" He rushed to his office to pack up his laptop computer.

RUSSELL SAT IN A RUNDOWN BAR ON THE edge of town and drank away the rest of the afternoon. He had let his family down again, and he didn't want to think about it. It wasn't his fault, he thought. Sometimes, he just got so confused.

Russell believed that ten years ago aliens had abducted him. He had been taken into their spaceship, where they performed painful experiments on him. He tried to explain what had happened, but no one would listen. Instead, people laughed and made fun of him. Even his wife thought he had gone crazy. That's when he started to drink.

Ever since the abduction, Russell's mind wandered off all of the time and he couldn't think clearly. Every night he dreamed about getting back at the horrible creatures.

Just as Russell was about to finish his fourth beer, the room started to shake and rumble and then it slowly went dark. It looked like the lights in a movie theater slowly dimming away, and it felt like an earthquake. But it was the middle of the afternoon and this was no quake. The spaceship was passing by on its way to Los Angeles.

Russell ran out of the bar and squinted up into the sky to see the monstrous thing rolling past him above. "They're back!" he said. He almost sounded happy. He knew it was only a matter of time before the creepy little creatures returned. *At last,* he thought, *people will believe me.*

Russell's kids saw it, too. The fireball was hanging in the sky, rolling toward their motor home and casting a shadow as big as the valley below.

"Oh, my God," Alicia said as she grabbed Troy's hand.

ALL OVER THE COUNTRY, THE SHADOWS OF the approaching spaceships were engulfing the cities in darkness. It was a terrifying thing for people to see. They were creeping over the United States' most beloved buildings and monuments: the Empire State Building, the George Washington Bridge, the Washington Monument, the Lincoln Memorial, the Capitol Building. The White House. The Statue of Liberty. America's symbols of liberty, freedom and peace were all being drenched in the huge, looming shadows of ships that were holding visitors from another world.

People were running in terror through their offices and down busy city streets, across grassy parks and through neighbor's yards. Panicked drivers were crashing into one another everywhere on the roads. Everyone was trying to get away from the monstrous black disks. They couldn't, though.

It was like watching flies struggling to escape from a spider when they are already caught in its web.

AT THE WHITE HOUSE, PRESIDENT WHITMORE was planning his next move. He was talking on the phone to the president of Russia, who sounded very tired and very nervous. He wanted President Whitmore's assurance that Russia and the United States were in this together. That they would fight together against whatever hung in the sky if they had to.

"Of course, Mr. President," said President Whitmore, "you have my word. . . . Yes . . . yes . . . okay . . . *Das vedanya.*" The president hung up.

"It's here!" Connie said as she rushed to the window.

Patricia ran into the room and jumped into her father's arms. "Daddy!" she yelled.

"It's okay, Patty," the president said. He held his daughter tight.

The room began to rumble and shake. Pictures on the mantel broke as they fell onto the floor. The room went dark. The ship was here. It was directly above the White House.

A secret service man moved toward the president. "We have to go, Mr. President," he said.

Everyone stepped out onto the balcony to get a better look at what had just blacked out the sun above them. The sight was magnificent and hideous at the same time.

"My God, what do we do now?" Connie whispered.

"I've got to address the nation," President Whitmore said. "There are a lot of scared people out there right now."

"Yeah," agreed Connie, "I'm one of them."

AROUND THE WORLD, PEOPLE WERE TRYING to get away from the three dozen spaceships that were headed for their cities. Places like Beijing, China; Berlin, Germany; Tel Aviv, Israel; and Yokohama, Japan. People from every race, religion, and walk of life who on any other day had nothing in common did today. They were all afraid of the unknown that hung in the sky like a giant question mark.

IN A QUIET SUBURBAN NEIGHBORHOOD IN Los Angeles, the sun was shining brightly, birds were chirping, and a gentle breeze was blowing. It was still early morning, and there was no sign of anything out of the ordinary. Some people who had seen news reports were packing up their things just in case, but most people were sleeping in on this beautiful summer morning. They didn't know yet that a fifteen-mile-wide spaceship was headed their way.

Dylan was just getting home from his slumber party. When he got out of the car, he looked up the street and saw a huge dark shadow headed his way. He ran in the house as fast as his six-year-old legs would carry him. He ran down the hallway and threw open the door to his mom's bedroom.

"Mommy, look at! It's a spaceship!" said Dylan. He had seen them on cartoons and knew exactly what they looked like.

Jasmine sat up in bed and rubbed her eyes. It was dark now because of the quickly approaching craft. She thought it was only five in the morning, the light was so dim. "It's too early, baby," she said as she laid her head back down on her pillow. Dylan ran back out to the living room to check on the situation.

Just then, the darkened room began to rumble. Jasmine assumed it was a little earthquake, like the kind they got in California all of the time. It wasn't enough to get upset about, but now she was definitely awake. She could hear her dog, Boomer, whimpering in the kitchen for breakfast, and Dylan was making all sorts of buzzing and shooting noises as he played with his toys. And then there was Steve, the noisiest of them all. Steve was Jasmine's boyfriend and a captain in the marine corps. Jasmine laid in bed and listened to Steve play shoot-out with Dylan and talk baby-talk to the dog. It made her smile. She was so happy when he was there.

Jasmine put on her robe and made her way into the living room. Steve was lying on his back trying to wrestle his sneaker away from Boomer while Dylan climbed all over him yelling, "I'm attackin' you, you alien. You're my prisoner."

When she walked in and gave them all a motherly disapproving face, Steve said, "Oh, sorry, hon. Did we wake you?"

"Oh no, no," Jasmine pulled Dylan off Steve and onto her lap, "what made you think that?"

Every time Steve looked at Jasmine, he couldn't stop staring at her. She was so beautiful and so sweet. She was everything he had always wanted and never had. Steve had been spending as much time as possible with her lately, and he was even thinking of asking her to marry him.

This was the first time anything or anyone had meant more to Steve than his career. He was one of the best pilots that the marines had. Whenever a new plane would come in, he would be the first to volunteer to fly it. He had to be the best at everything he tried, because he was preparing to fly the most important thing America had to offer. Steve wanted to be an astronaut. And until now, that's all he ever thought about.

But now he spent a lot of time thinking about Jasmine and Dylan, too. Part of him was worried that he was getting too distracted. Eventually, though, he had decided there was room in his life for both his career and the girl of his dreams.

"So, Steve," said Jasmine with a wink, "let's go see this spaceship."

Dylan had a vivid imagination, and Steve and Jasmine always liked to encourage him. Little did they know that Dylan was not pretending today.

Jasmine lazily flopped her slippered feet over to the coffee pot and poured herself and Steve a cup. She noticed that the plates in the cupboard were still rattling. "Long earthquake," she said to herself, and walked out to join Steve in the driveway, where he was scanning the newspaper.

Steve looked up from his paper to see the next-door neighbors quickly throw their belongings in the car, jump in, and take off speeding down the street. "Wimps," Steve said out loud. "Can't even take a little earthquake."

Just then, he saw it. The neighbors were no wimps. The huge spaceship was rolling over the neighborhood. It was so enormous Steve couldn't see where it ended. Jasmine ran to Steve and held on tight to his arm. Both of them stood there speechless, with their jaws dropped, as the ship took over the entire sky above them. They noticed the details of the underside as it continued to roll past them. The bottom was flat and had a pattern that looked like an enormous gray daisy with eight long petals.

The craft seemed to be headed for downtown. Dylan ran out to join his mom and Steve. He aimed his green plastic alien-zapper gun at the sky. "Pow pow!"

BEFORE DAVID RUSHED OUT OF THE Compact Cable building, he stopped to listen to the news one more time. He wanted to see if anyone had figured out his new theory about the signal disturbance. The offices were completely empty now.

The reporter in Washington, D.C., said: "Officials here at the Pentagon have just confirmed what CNN has been reporting. Additional airships, like the one hovering directly above me, have arrived over thirty-six major cities around the globe. No one I've spoken with here is willing to make an official comment, but speaking off the record, several people have expressed their frustration that our space defense systems failed to provide any kind of warning for us."

A map then came up on the screen showing all of the cities that now had a spaceship hovering over them. It was just as David had expected. From watching the news, it really didn't seem like anyone else had figured out what he now knew.

Whoever or whatever was inside these beastly disks was using the world's satellites to communicate their own signal to one another. This way, they could coordinate the placement of the spaceships all over the world simultaneously. David's mind was racing. If he could only figure out how to disable the signal, perhaps he could stop the invasion. He suddenly heard a voice coming from under one of the desks. It was Marty on the phone. He sounded as if he was about ready to cry.

"I know Ma, just try and stay calm!"

"It's gonna be okay—yeah—just stay inside—okay—I'll call ya when I get to my place—okay . . . "

David interrupted, "Tell her to get out of town!"

"Why? What happened?" asked Marty.

"Just do it!" yelled David.

Marty knew that if David was this upset, he should do exactly what he said. "Listen, Ma? Pack up your things and head for Aunt Ester's—don't argue with me, just go!" He slammed down the phone and ran after David. "David, why'd I just send my mother to Atlanta? David, talk to me, please!"

David stopped to explain to Marty. "Remember when I told you about the signal inside the signal?"

Marty looked confused. "Not really," he said.

"It's a countdown," said David.

"A countdown? A countdown to what?"

"Think about it. It's just like in chess. First you strategically position your pieces, and then when the timing is right, you strike. You see?" David pointed to the map on the screen. "They're positioning themselves over the world's most important cities and using the signal to coordinate their attack. The signal is getting shorter and shorter. In approximately six hours, the signal will disappear and the countdown will be over."

Marty didn't understand completely, but he was beside himself. "And then what?" He was biting the nails on his shaking hands.

"Checkmate."

"Oh my God, oh my God," Marty kept saying over and over. He ran out of the building and hopped in his car. If David was right, there was no time to lose.

David picked up the phone and dialed Connie's

office. One of her aides answered and said she was unavailable. David could see her on his television screen standing to the side of the podium where the president was addressing the nation. "It's her husband," David said, "this is an emergency."

The aide handed the phone to Connie. She didn't look happy to hear that David was on the phone.

"What is it, David?" asked Connie.

"Connie, listen, you have to get out of there," said David. "Please get out of the White House, leave Washington, you don't understand how—" He was rambling and stuttering because he knew she would hang up at any moment, and he had to let her know what he knew.

"David, I'm a little busy right now. In case you haven't noticed, we're in a bit of a crisis," Connie said, and then hung up.

They had argued many times about her choice to move to Washington to serve the president. Connie only thought David was bringing the sore subject up once again. She didn't realize that he was trying to warn her. David knew it wouldn't do any good to phone again, because she would never take the call. He was so frustrated. He turned to the TV to hear the rest of the president's speech.

"My staff and I plan to remain here at the White House . . ." said President Whitmore.

"No!" David yelled at the TV. He grabbed his bike and his laptop and rushed out. He had to warn them to get out from under the belly of the dark monster in the sky.

Outside, the worst traffic jam in history was taking place. Everywhere David looked, cars were crashing into one another and horns were blaring. Some people were walking their way out of town and making much better progress than the people in the cars. David wove his way through the stopped cars on his bicycle. He was headed for his father's house.

As David coasted up to a row of brownstone houses, he had to swerve at the last second to avoid a mattress that someone had pitched out of a second-story window. Everywhere he looked, people were packing up their cars to head out of town. He ran up to Julius' door and knocked.

Suddenly, David found the barrel of a shotgun pointed straight at his nose. Julius hid behind the door.

"Whoa, Pops, it's me!" He pushed the gun out of his face.

Julius lowered the gun and peeked out from the door. "Did you see on the news? People are looting already! I swear before God, if anyone tries to break in here, I'll shoot 'em! Vultures!"

"Dad, calm down. Do you still have the Plymouth?" asked David.

"Yeah, what do you care? You don't have a license," Julius said.

David walked into the house, "That's okay, you're driving."

"I'm driving! What? Where?"

After a quick explanation, David and Julius were packed in the Plymouth and headed for Washington, D.C.

STEVE HAD CHANGED INTO HIS OFFICER'S uniform and was preparing to head back down to El Toro. He had received the "yellow alert" message on the TV that requested all military personnel to report to their posts. He didn't want to leave Jasmine, but part of him was anxious to find out what was going on. Jasmine didn't understand why he had to leave.

"You could say you didn't hear the announcement," she offered.

"Come on, Jas, you know I can't do that," said Steve, putting the last of his things into his duffel bag. "Now, I've gotta go. I've got to report to El Toro."

"But you promised to be with us this weekend," Jasmine whined. She knew she was being unreasonable, but she was afraid.

"Well, things have changed just a little bit! Jas, why are you acting like this?" asked Steve.

"Why?" *How could he ask that question?* Jasmine thought. She marched over to the window and pointed to where the sky used to be. "That's why! I'm scared to death, Steve!"

Steve walked over to the window and put his arms around her. "Look, I really don't think they flew ninety billion light years to come down here and start a fight." Steve kissed her cheek. He really meant it, too. Steve wasn't the kind of person to get scared or nervous about anything. Besides, although his military training taught him to be suspicious of any potential aggressor, he didn't automatically assume that aliens would be evil like they were in the movies. Maybe they were coming to learn from us or to teach us, he thought. Steve was excited about all of the possibilities and especially how this visit might affect future space exploration for the United States.

Jasmine followed Steve out to his convertible Mustang, where Dylan was sitting in the driver's seat making *vroom-vroom* noises. She wanted to tell Steve that she loved him and to be careful, but she lost her nerve. Jasmine was finally getting her life together, and for the first time she had felt like everything was working out. But now, it seemed as if this spaceship was screwing everything up. She knew Steve had to return to his base, but it was hard to accept that in a moment of crisis he was leaving her.

He held out a little glass dolphin that had been sitting on Jasmine's night table. She loved dolphins and had them all over her house.

"Can I take this with me?" asked Steve. "I'll bring it back."

She smiled and nodded. She wanted to believe that he would be back.

"Oh, I almost forgot," Steve said as he reached into the back of his car. He pulled out a paper bag full of long sticks covered in brightly colored paper. They were like oversized bottle rockets and had the name FyreStix printed on the side. "Here Dylan, like I promised. But you have to be really careful, okay? We'll shoot them off together when I get back," said Steve.

"Wow, cool!" said Dylan. Jasmine shot Steve a "gee, thanks a lot" look of disapproval. She was too nervous to be upset, though. She was stalling Steve, trying to think of something to say. Finally, Steve spoke up.

"Look, why don't you get some things together and come down to the base. You and Dylan can stay down there with me tonight, okay?"

"Really? You mean it?" asked Jasmine.

"Of course I mean it," Steve said. "But I will have to tell all of my other girlfriends that they can't come down tonight." Steve smiled. He loved to tease Jasmine. She punched him lightly on the arm.

"You know, you're not as charming as you think you are, sir," said Jasmine.

"Yes, I am," Steve said and flashed her his best smile.

"Dumbo ears," she said.

"Chicken legs," he shot back as he hopped into the car. Jasmine lifted Dylan out of the car, gave Steve a final kiss, and stood watching as he drove away. She couldn't wait until tonight.

"I'll take these," she told Dylan as she removed the FyreStix from his hands and walked back into the house.

"Ahh, Mom!" Dylan sighed.

AT THE MOTOR HOME PARK, NERVOUS people were milling about everywhere, talking and planning. Miguel had moved to their motor home's rooftop, lugging the TV set with him, in an attempt to get better reception. He hadn't heard from Russell since their confrontation at the field that afternoon, which was exactly what Miguel expected. *He's probably off getting drunk,* he thought.

Miguel looked across the horizon toward Los Angeles, where he could see the edge of the spaceship sitting over the outer edge of the city. He then focused his attention back on the news to see if there was any place safe to go. He had to figure out what would be best for his brother and sister. As he flipped through the channels, he thought about what he would say to Russell to get rid of him. Suddenly, he got a glimpse of Russell on a news report. He was in handcuffs and being escorted by two policemen to a squad car. His face was bright red and he was screaming at the camera. Miguel stared at the screen, horrified, as he listened.

The newscaster reported: "In lighter news, a local crop duster was arrested today for littering the valley with fliers to warn us all of the aliens inside the ship."

They cut back to Russell. "You people better do something! They'll kill us all! I was abducted ten years ago, they did all kinds of tests on me, no one believed me, but you've got to believe me now! We're doomed if we don't do something!"

The reporter looked like she was about to laugh. "The man, identified as Russell Casse, is being held at the Lancaster Police—"

Miguel quickly changed the channel when his little brother Troy joined him on the roof. "Whatcha watchin'?" he asked.

"Oh, nothing." Miguel was trying to hide how upset he was. "Hey, Troy, do you remember Uncle Hector in Tucson?"

"Yeah, he's got that Sega Saturn CD, sixty-four-bit," said Troy.

"Right." Miguel paused. "How would you feel if we went and lived with him for a while?"

"That'd be cool," said Troy, "but what about Dad?"

Miguel ignored his question. "Pack up. We're going." Miguel jumped up and headed down the ladder. Troy continued to yell after Miguel. "Hey, what about Dad, Miguel? Answer me." But Miguel was gone.

The plan was in motion. He'd round up his sister, pack up their few things, and drive the motor home to Tucson. He wasn't even sure if Uncle Hector lived there anymore, but he was the only relative Miguel knew.

The windows in the car where Alicia was sitting were too steamy to see through. She was in the world's longest lip-lock with a boy who lived in the nearby town. He was a little bit older than Alicia. He had a part-time job and a car, and that was all that mattered to her. To Alicia this meant that he could possibly take her away from her miserable life in the cramped motor home with her two brothers and crazy, drunk dad. She wasn't willing to go all the way with the boy, but every night he tried his hardest to change her mind. Tonight, he had a new tactic.

"This could be our last night on earth," he said as he slid his hand under her shirt. "You don't want to die a virgin, do you?"

Alicia squirmed away from his exploring hand. This was getting a little too intense for her, so she tried to set him off balance. "What makes you think I'm still a virgin?" she said.

It worked. The boy stopped everything. Maybe he wasn't the most experienced one in the car. Just then, the door swung open and Miguel hoisted Alicia out of the car.

"Stop it, Miguel!" she shouted.

"Come on Alicia, we're going," Miguel said.

"Right! I'm not going anywhere with you," she said.

Miguel sneered at the boy, who sat dumbstruck in the car.

Alicia was angry with Miguel for bossing her around like that. After all, he was only two years older.

But secretly, she was relieved that, once again, she had escaped from a sticky situation.

Two hours later, Miguel fired up the motor home. The Casse kids were headed for Tucson. Just as they began to pull out of the park, a car came to a dusty stop in front of them and out stepped Russell. "Thanks, man!" he shouted to the driver as the car pulled away. He saw the motor home all packed up and running. Miguel got out and walked toward him.

"Hey, Miguel! You read my mind! Let's get as far away from these things as we can!" Russell was stumbling toward the motor home and Miguel stepped in front of him.

"They let you out?" Miguel asked.

"Sure tootin' they did! They've got bigger fish to fry now, believe you me! Hop in and let's go!"

"We're leaving without you, Russell. We don't want you around anymore," Miguel said.

"What are you talking about?" asked Russell.

"We're tired of picking up after you, Russell. Carrying around your dead weight. We're going to Tucson to live with Uncle Hector."

"Hector! Ha!" Russell laughed. "You're not going anywhere. I'm still your father."

At that point, Miguel lost his cool. "No, you're not! You're just some fool who married my mother! You're nothing to me!" Miguel was afraid of what Russell might do. If he was drunk, he might fly into a real rage.

"Oh." Russell straightened his dopey-looking cap and let the harsh words sink in. "I see. So, what about Troy?"

"What about Troy? For once in your life, Russell, why don't you think about what's best for him? Who takes care of him? Who has to beg for money to buy him medicine when you screw up? Who? Me! That's who!" Miguel could have gone on, but the sound of breaking glass stopped him.

"Stop it!" screamed Troy through his tears. "I'm not a baby! I don't need your stupid medicine and I don't need you!" He broke another medicine bottle on the rocky dirt before Miguel reached him.

"Troy! Stop it! Do you know how much this stuff costs? Now what are we gonna do?" Miguel was ready to cry, too. He knew he'd lost to Russell. He slowly walked back to the motor home and climbed inside with Alicia.

"Come on Troy-boy." Russell put his arm around his young sobbing son. "Let's go."

AS JULIUS CRUISED ALONG THE HIGHWAY AT fifty-five miles per hour, David sat silently beside him. He was trying with all of his might not to scream, "Dad, for God sakes, hurry up!" He knew that, for Julius, this was hurrying. The old man usually never took the old Plymouth past thirty-five.

On their side of the road, the highway was

completely empty. The road heading out of town was in total gridlock.

"The whole world's trying to get out of Washington," smirked Julius. "We're the only schmucks trying to get in."

"We could go a little faster, Pops. I mean, I don't think anyone's writing any speeding tickets today."

"Hey, any faster and the engine will blow up! Trust me! I know," said Julius.

The other thing that was making the trip seem five million miles long was Julius' nonstop chatter. He went from politics to neighbor gossip to what he had for dinner for the last three nights to why David wasn't dating anyone. Julius was also still puzzled by what David hoped to accomplish with this trip. He started in on that subject again as they neared the final stretch into Washington.

"It's the White House for Pete's sake, you can't just walk up and ring the bell," said Julius. "You think they don't know what you know? They know, trust me, they know."

"They don't know this," said David.

"And you're going to educate them?" Julius turned his whole body to face David. "Tell me something. If you're so smart, how come it took you eight years at MIT to become a cable repair man?"

This hurt David, but he wasn't going to get drawn into a fight with Julius right now. "Dad, please," was all he said. Julius was on a roll.

"All I'm saying is they've got people who handle these kinds of things. If they want HBO, they'll call you."

David stared at the car ceiling and smiled weakly.

As they reached the top of the hill that led into Washington, both men stared at the sky ahead. They were looking at the belly of a giant disk that looked exactly like the one they had seen in New York. The city lights were just bright enough to show the massive gray outlines of the ship's dark flower design. For the first time on the long journey, even Julius was speechless. After a moment, he cleared his throat.

"David, what do you say we turn around. Let's go somewhere where there isn't a spaceship. How's that for an idea, hmm?"

"Dad, please, we're almost there now," said David. He felt he needed to get to the White House even faster now that he had seen the spaceship. He grabbed his laptop from the backseat and quickly booted it up. From a plastic file sleeve, he extracted a CD-ROM and stuffed it into the drive.

"What's that for?" Julius had only seen a computer a few times and didn't quite understand what they could do.

"On this CD, Dad, is every phone book in America," said David.

"You don't say?"

David nodded.

"And you're going to try to find Constance in there?

What makes you think an important person like her would be listed?" Julius asked.

"She always keeps her portable phone listed for emergencies. The problem is figuring out what name it's under. I've tried C. Spano, Constance Spano, Spunky Spano . . ." David trailed off into thought.

"Spunky?" asked Julius.

"Oh, yeah, college nickname," said David.

"Cute," said Julius. "How about Levinson?"

"No, Dad, she didn't take my name when we were married. Why would she be using it now?" asked David. Julius just stared back at him. "Okay, I'll look for Constance Levinson." David typed. Up popped the phone number.

"So what do I know?" said Julius, and smiled a satisfied grin.

Just then, the piercing whine of a siren made them both look up. There was a police car headed straight for them, and it was leading hundreds of cars to the other side of the road—Julius and David's side of the road.

"Oy my God," said Julius as he punched the accelerator. He was darting and weaving back and forth between the cars racing straight for him.

David couldn't believe his eyes. *Is this the same man who wouldn't go past fifty-five miles per hour only a few minutes ago?* he thought. The tables had definitely turned now.

David kept yelling, "Slow down!" His face was as white as a sheet.

Julius jerked the car left to miss someone's front bumper and almost plowed head-on into a station wagon. Something inside him told him to keep moving. As car after car crashed around them, the two made their way to a freeway offramp to catch their breath.

Both were panting as if they had just sprinted a mile by the time it was over. David looked over at his father, who looked scared to death. "Nice driving, Pops," David said.

The two of them looked at each other and burst out laughing. For a few moments they forgot about getting to Washington and simply sat there in the car giggling their heads off as the huge dark ship loomed in the distance.

JASMINE DIDN'T KNOW HOW SHE HAD BEEN talked into working today. She had planned to go in just to pick up her paycheck before heading down to El Toro to meet Steve. But her boss, Mario, was at the bar and told her that she had better work her shift, or else. So she did. She put on her costume and walked out on stage to begin her dance. When she looked around the bar, though, she realized that there wasn't a single person in there who had any interest in the show. Everyone was glued to the updates of more arriving spaceships on the TV news. Jasmine felt like an idiot standing there, so she ran into the back to grab Dylan and Boomer and get out of there.

Backstage she saw that her friend Tiffany was also glued to a little black-and-white set. She was staring at a live picture of crowds of people who had gathered on the rooftops of the highest buildings in downtown Los Angeles. This put them directly under the center of the spaceship. People were dancing and celebrating the arrival of the visitors. Many of them held signs that said things like, "TAKE ME TO YOUR LEADER!" and "EXPERIMENT ON ME!" The news was hovering above in a helicopter. They were calling the people the "alien lovers."

"This is sooo cool, Jasmine," said Tiffany without taking her eyes off of the screen, "and you thought I was nuts."

Jasmine glanced at the TV over Tiffany's shoulder. "You're not thinking of joining those idiots, are you?"

"I'm going up there as soon as I get off," Tiffany said. She reached into her bag and pulled out a bright yellow sign that looked like a four-year-old had made it. In big green and blue letters it said, "WELCOME, MAKE YOURSELVES AT HOME!"

Jasmine gave Tiffany her best motherly stare. She even shook her finger at her. "Tiffany, I don't want you to go up there. Now, promise me you won't!"

Tiffany didn't really have a mother and Jasmine was always looking out for her. But to hear she couldn't go join the alien lovers broke her heart. "Oh, man!"

"Tiffany, promise me!"

"All right, I promise." She pouted.

"Good, all right, I'm out of here," said Jasmine, and left the dressing room.

She went to get Dylan and Boomer, who were waiting in Mario's office. "Come on, guys, let's go!" Dylan jumped into his mom's arms and they were on their way, until Mario walked in the room.

"Hey, what's your kid *and* dog doing here?" Mario yelled.

"Why don't you try and find a baby-sitter today!" snapped Jasmine.

"Where do you think you're going? If you leave, you're fired!"

Jasmine looked at him and looked at the door. "Nice working with you, Mario!" She walked out and Dylan waved good-bye to the speechless man.

WHEN STEVE ENTERED THE LOCKER ROOM AT El Toro, he found the pilots in his squad in a pretty good mood, considering the circumstances. The squad's official nickname was the Black Knights, and they were known throughout the country as some of the best tactical pilots in the entire armed forces. Steve was the natural leader of the group. Everyone greeted him when he walked in.

Jimmy was Steve's flight partner and best friend. He was kicking back with both feet on the top of a locker door and his arms behind his head. "Where have you been, Captain?" Jimmy tossed a towel in Steve's general direction.

"You guys could have started without me, you know," said Steve, "but no, you all have been just sittin' around on your butts using me as an excuse."

"Yeah, so what's wrong with that?" asked Jimmy.

Steve laughed and walked toward his own locker to put away his things. Jimmy followed him. "This is serious, man, they've put every employee on 'yellow alert.'"

Steve opened his locker and saw that the mail had been delivered. He flipped through the stack until he came to a large envelope with the word NASA in the upper left-hand corner. He stared at it for a moment before handing it to Jimmy. "You open it," he said, "I can't take it."

"Wuss," said Jimmy as he ripped into the envelope and pulled out a letter. He started to read aloud. "Dear Captain Steven Hiller, United States Marine Corps, blah blah blah, we regret to inform you that despite your outstanding record . . ." Jimmy trailed off. He felt really sorry for his pal. "Listen, Steve, I've told you this a hundred times. If you want to get anywhere in this world, it's not enough to be the best. If you want to fly the space shuttle, you've got to learn to kiss some butt." Jimmy was trying to lighten the mood, but so far Steve wasn't smiling. "So to really kiss some butt, you have to get into the right butt-kissing position. . . ." Jimmy knelt down on one knee in front of Steve. "See, this puts you at the perfect level with the butt that needs to be kissed."

Steve couldn't help but laugh at his funny friend. He turned to stuff his jacket into his locker and a little box fell out of his pocket.

"What's this?" Jimmy opened the box and found a diamond ring in the shape of a dolphin. Steve was slightly embarrassed. "Is this an engagement ring?" asked Jimmy.

"Jasmine has a thing for dolphins," Steve said shyly as he tried to grab the ring back. Jimmy held it out of reach.

Just then, a group of their squad walked by and saw Jimmy kneeling in front of Steve with the ring in his hand. It looked like a proposal was about to happen between the two men. Jimmy suddenly realized what everyone was thinking and quickly jumped to his feet.

THE STREETS SURROUNDING THE WHITE House were cluttered with police and tanks and military men armed with rifles. There was also a group of protesters who were upset about the military presence. They were afraid that the military would overreact to the visitors and maybe even provoke them. They were carrying signs that said things like "TRY PEACE!" and "VIOLENCE IS WRONG!"

Julius drove through the whole mess like he had

the president of the United States in the back of his car. He didn't wait for clearance from anyone, and surprisingly, no one stopped him. He rolled to a stop right in front of the White House lawn.

"Okay, we're here," said Julius. "You want to ring the bell, or should I?"

David let the sarcasm slide. He opened his cellular phone and dialed Connie's number. "Perfect, she's on the phone."

"Perfect? The line is busy and you can't reach her?" asked Julius.

"No, this way I can triangulate her exact position in the White House at this very moment."

"You can do that?"

David gave Julius a shot of sarcasm right back. "All cable repairmen can, Pops."

INSIDE THE WHITE HOUSE, CONNIE WAS IN one of the hallways taking care of some personal business. She had called her neighbor and asked her to take her cat with her when she left town. She hung up and the phone rang again. "Constance," she said.

"Connie, don't hang up," David said.

"How did you get this number?" Connie asked rather nastily.

"There's a window right in front of you. Walk over to it," said David.

Connie turned around and, sure enough, there was a window. She pulled back the lace curtains. "All right," she said into the phone, "what am I looking at?"

He didn't need to answer. As soon as she looked at the street she saw David standing on the hood of Julius' car waving his arms. "How does he do that?" she said to herself.

A secret serviceman quickly ran up to him and helped him down off of the car. He took the phone from David's hand. "Who is this?" the man asked into the receiver.

"This is Constance Spano," she said. "The man is my husband. It's all right." She wasn't sure if it actually was all right, but she didn't want David to get arrested. *Now what?* she thought.

AT ANDREW'S AIR FORCE BASE IN Washington, D.C., a huge crowd of reporters had gathered along with hundreds of military personnel and government officials. Everyone was anxiously awaiting earth's first attempt to make contact with the hovering spacecraft. The mission was being called Operation Welcome Wagon.

A sixty-foot-long, thirty-foot-high, eighteen-ton piece of machinery called an Apache helicopter had been rigged with a giant steel frame so it could hold two giant light boards. The plan was for the lights to flash on and off in a binary sequence. The scientists who designed "Welcome Wagon" figured that the best chance of communicating with the visitors would be through math.

A thousand cameras began to flash when the long helicopter blades began to turn. Reporters shouted questions to the soldiers and press officers who held the crowd back. Millions of people around the world were watching on the edge of their seats.

"What you see behind me," one reporter yelled to the camera, "is an Apache attack helicopter that has been refitted with synchronized light boards. Pentagon officials hope these lights will be our first step in communicating with the alien craft."

As soon as the blades were at full speed, the ground crew moved away and the pilot carefully lifted off. Several smaller helicopters with cameras trailed behind the Apache as it headed for the belly of the craft. People everywhere followed the scene on their television screens. Even in the White House, all work stopped as everyone watched the TV screen.

"Where are we?" asked President Whitmore as he walked into the room.

Everyone snapped to attention and General Grey answered him, "We're in the air, Mr. President. They should arrive in six minutes."

Down the White House hall, Julius and David Levinson stepped out of the elevator and followed Constance to the Oval Office. Julius felt very self-conscious about his appearance. He never actually believed that they would make it inside the White House.

"If I had known I was going to meet the president, I woulda worn a tie! Look at me!" Julius said as he looked down at his wrinkled trousers. "I look like a slob-ola!"

"You two wait right here," said Constance as she showed them into the office. "I'll tell the president you need to speak with him, David, but I'm not sure how happy he's going to be to see you."

"I know," said David, "we're wasting time. He's never going to listen to me."

"Why? Why wouldn't he listen?" asked Julius.

"Because the last time David saw him, he punched him in the face," said Connie.

"You did *what*? You punched the president?" Julius could not believe his ears.

"He wasn't the president then," said David.

Julius still couldn't believe it. "How could you punch the president? Oy my God!"

Constance added, "David thought I was having an affair, which I wasn't, so he punched him." She turned to leave the room. She had to smile on her way down the hall. She could still hear Julius yelling at his son.

Connie was nervous at pulling her boss away from the conference room where Operation Welcome Wagon was being monitored. Especially to speak with her unpredictable husband. But David had managed to convince her that he was on to something big with the discovery of this signal within a signal. She took a deep breath and walked in. She whispered into the president's ear and he got up to follow her out of the room.

"You're leaving *now*?" Secretary Nimziki asked loud enough for everyone to hear. He was always trying to make the president look bad.

As soon as they were out of the room, Connie said, "Ughh! How can you stand that guy?"

"He ran the CIA for years. He knows a lot of important secrets, which can come in pretty handy," said the president. They walked into the Oval Office. The president looked at David and was immediately angry. "Oh, Connie, I don't believe this!" He started to head for the door.

"Please, Tom, just give David a moment," said Connie. "He's convinced he's found something that can really help us."

Julius tried to break the tension in the room. He walked up to the president and extended his hand. "Julius Levinson, Mr. President. It's an honor to meet you. We'll only take a moment of your time."

David decided to give it a try. "I know why we have satellite disruption."

"Go on," President Whitmore said.

"These ships have positioned themselves all over the globe." David walked over to the desk and drew a circle on a notepad. "If you wanted to coordinate the actions of ships all over the world, you couldn't send one signal to every place at the same time." He drew lines between the ships to show how the curve of the earth would block their signals.

"You're talking about line of sight," said the president.

"Exactly," said David. "The curve of the earth prevents it, so a signal would have to be relayed using satellites in order to reach all of the ships." David drew a pair of satellites around his drawing of the earth. "They've put a signal inside our signal, and it's actually—"

Before David could finish, someone walked into the room and said, "Excuse me Mr. President, the Apache is ready to send the message."

President Whitmore turned on the television in his office. So far David hadn't told him anything he didn't already know from intelligence reports from Space Command. He was losing his patience.

The Apache came to the front of the spaceship and turned on its light boards. The message that was being sent in flashing lights was not understandable to the humans watching the screen. The president turned his attention back to David. "So they're communicating with one another using our satellites, correct?"

David turned his laptop screen around and showed the president the graphic he had created. "This wave is a measurement of the signal. When I first found it, it was recycling itself every twenty minutes. Now it's down to three. It seems to be fading out, but the power is still the same. I think it's a countdown."

The president stared back at the TV, lost in thought. The Apache looked like a pesky mosquito buzzing around the nose of a giant.

"Mr. President," David started, "these things are using our own satellites against us to send out a countdown, and the clock is ticking."

"When will the signal disappear?" asked the president.

David showed his countdown ticker on his laptop screen. "Thirty-one minutes."

The president was afraid to admit it, but this information made sense to him. If David was right about the countdown, it was time to spring into action. He nodded his head and walked out of the room, down the hall, and into the briefing room with a whole new battle plan.

"General Grey, I want you to coordinate a country-wide evacuation of the cities. Get as many people out as possible in the next twenty-five minutes," President Whitmore said.

"What the heck is going on?" Secretary Nimziki began.

"And get that helicopter away from the spaceship. Call them back immediately."

General Grey picked up the direct line to Andrews Air Force Base and relayed the orders.

President Whitmore addressed the room. "We're evacuating the White House, effective immediately. Let me have two choppers on the lawn in five minutes.

"THIRTY-SIX SHIPS,
POSSIBLE ENEMIES,
ARE HEADED THIS WAY,
MR. PRESIDENT.
WHETHER WE LIKE IT OR
NOT, WE MUST GO TO
DEFCON THREE."

"MARTY, QUIT WASTING
TIME AND GET OUT OF
TOWN RIGHT NOW."

"MY GOD! MY GOD! IT'S DESTROYING EVERYTHING. WIDENING—"

"ALL SATELLITES, MICROWAVE, AND GROUND COMMUNICATIONS WITH THE TARGET CITIES ARE GONE. WE BELIEVE WE'RE LOOK-ING AT A TOTAL LOSS."

"MOMMY, WHAT HAPPENED?"

"I DON'T KNOW, DYLAN. MOMMY DOESN'T KNOW."

"HA! NEVER ANY SPACESHIPS RECOVERED BY THE GOVERNMENT?"

"THIS, LADIES AND GENTLEMEN, IS WHAT WE AFFECTIONATELY
REFER TO DOWN HERE AS THE FREAK SHOW."

"LISTEN, DOCTOR, MY BOY IS VERY SICK. HE NEEDS IMMEDIATE ATTENTION."

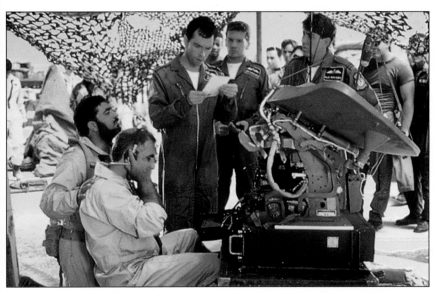

"IT'S FROM THE AMERICANS. THEY WANT TO ORGANIZE A COUNTEROFFENSIVE."

"WE'VE DONE WHAT WE COULD
TO DISGUISE IT. THE MISSILE'S
NOSE CONE IS GOING TO PRO-
TRUDE SOMEWHAT."

"I'M A PILOT, WILL. I BELONG IN
THE AIR."

"NO, NO, NO. WE CAN'T GO YET. CIGARS, MAN. I GOTTA FIND SOME CIGARS."

"I HAVE A CONFESSION TO MAKE. I'M NOT REAL BIG ON FLYING."

Somebody go downstairs and get my daughter." Advisors and staff began to quickly bustle about the room. Then someone yelled, "They're responding!" Everyone's eyes went back to the TV monitor.

A beam of green light shot from the base of the tower at the center of the huge floating disk. It was aimed straight for the Apache helicopter. The Apache moved back slightly. Then a horrible screeching began as two of the enormous plates on the craft began to wind their way open. As the panels pulled apart, the light from inside the big ship overpowered the light board on the Apache. The men inside the helicopter shielded their eyes and tried to maintain their positions. When the president's order to end the mission reached the helicopters, the pilot came on the radio. "We have received orders to abort Operation Welcome Wa—"

The pilot didn't finish. A spike of white light shot through the green light, across the night sky and burst the helicopters into a billion tiny bits. Then the light was gone. The armor plates of the ship squealed shut and everything was dark again.

MARILYN WHITMORE SAT IN HER HOTEL ROOM in Los Angeles in stunned silence at what she had just seen on the TV. She had been packing up the last of her things while she watched Operation Welcome Wagon, and now she couldn't move. The television was replaying the explosion again and again in slow motion. She felt so awful for the pilots and their families. The worst part, though, was knowing that there was no chance these aliens were friendly after what she had just seen. She knew in her heart that the world was going to have to fight to defend itself.

"Excuse me, Mrs. Whitmore?" a Secret Service man walked into her room. "I have direct orders to evacuate you from Los Angeles as quickly as possible, ma'am. There's a helicopter waiting for you on the roof."

"Okay," Mrs. Whitmore collected herself, "let's move."

The helicopter was already warming up as they reached the rooftop. Mrs. Whitmore took a long look at the whirring blades and little cabin. After what she had just seen, she wasn't exactly excited about getting into one of those things and flying beneath the horrible ship. But what choice did she have? she thought.

As she looked out across the city, she noticed a curious thing. On the tops of all the buildings surrounding hers, she could see people dancing and cheering. They were holding signs and pointing at the ship.

They were what the news was calling the "alien lovers."

JASMINE, DYLAN, AND BOOMER WERE GOING nowhere fast. Along with everyone else in Los Angeles, they were sitting still in the fast lane on the freeway. Jasmine looked all around. No one was going anywhere. At the moment, she happened to be in the middle of a tunnel, and for some reason, that really gave her the creeps. On the radio, the announcer told everyone to try and avoid the freeways because of the heavy traffic.

"Gee, thanks for the tip," Jasmine said back at the radio. At the rate they were going, she wouldn't make it to El Toro to see Steve until next week.

THE PRESIDENT AND HIS GROUP WERE headed for the White House lawn where two choppers were ready to take them to safety. With Patricia in one arm, and Connie and General Grey to each side, he quickly made his way on board.

"Is my wife in the air?" President Whitmore yelled over the noise of the helicopters.

"She will be shortly," said General Grey.

Everyone quickly settled into their seats. The military guards had stopped David and Julius from boarding the helicopter, even though there was enough room. Connie felt a little panicked as she looked at the two of them standing on the lawn like abandoned puppies.

"Tom," she said as she looked at the two of them. She couldn't believe she was asking the president to bring along David given their history, but she couldn't ignore them, either.

"It's okay," said the president to the guard, "let them aboard."

The door was lowered and the men were brought on board. Before he hit the seat, David already had his laptop up and running. He was checking on the quickly approaching end of the countdown.

11:07, 11:06, 11:05 . . .

As the helicopter lifted, Connie looked down at the people left behind. Many of them had worked side by side with her for the past few years. Would she ever see them again? she wondered.

11:01, 11:00, 10:59 . . .

THE "ALIEN LOVERS'" PARTY WAS GOING FULL blast now. Tiffany ran up the last few flights of stairs and jumped right into the middle of the chaos like a giggling child doing a cannonball off a diving board into the middle of a crowded pool.

"I can't believe I'm really here!" she squealed. She felt bad about breaking her promise to Jasmine, but this might be a once in a lifetime thing, she thought. If Tiffany had missed it, she would have never forgiven herself.

She looked around the rooftop. "What a bunch of freaks! I love it!" she said. All around her were old people and young people. Some were punks and some were hippies carrying signs and screaming things like, "Welcome back, man!" Some people had even put on alien costumes. As soon as Tiffany was done taking in the crazy-looking crowd, she took a good look at the ship above them. It was so close, Tiffany thought she could feel its power over her. The surface was actually very lumpy. The lumps were warehouse-sized boxes and docks. It looked like someone had grabbed a city and turned it upside down.

Tiffany pulled her sign out and began to skip around with the rest of the alien lovers. A police helicopter swooped down over the top of the building. Over a bullhorn a voice told them to evacuate the city as quickly as possible. It said to leave the rooftops because it wasn't safe and they were trespassing. No one was buying it. Everyone started to wave their fists and boo at the police. This was their big moment. They weren't about to leave.

But all of the partying stopped when a tremendous screeching noise began above them. The huge plates on the bottom of the ship were slowly opening up. A bright greenish light poured through the openings. The petal-shaped plates moved away from one another, expanding away from the center. In the middle there was a long round tower that was slowly lowering itself closer to where the alien lovers stood. Suddenly it felt like they were being examined under a gigantic microscope.

"It's so pretty," was all Tiffany could say as she stared wide-eyed at the craft.

THE FIRST LADY'S HELICOPTER WAS MOVING at its top speed to get out of Los Angeles as quickly as possible. She had seen the spaceship open its petal-shaped armor and watched as the long tower in the center lowered itself. "Maybe it's some sort of observation tower," the pilot said. No one was quite sure, but it did make everyone on the helicopter want to get away as quickly as possible.

Then the green light coming out of the ship became much brighter, just as it had at Operation Welcome Wagon. The color was so peaceful, though, that people suddenly felt like everything was going to be all right. The parties on the rooftops fell silent. Everyone stared at the beautiful light.

AT ANDREWS AIR FORCE BASE, THE president and his group were quickly escorted across the tarmac and into the president's private jet, Air Force One. Everyone was taking David's countdown theory very seriously. There wasn't a moment to lose. The 747's turbine jet engines were already revved up to full power. The pilot hurled the plane down the runway as quickly as he could. David flipped open his laptop and watched the last few seconds of the countdown run out.

00:25, 00:24, 00:23 . . .

A WHITE LIGHT SHOT STRAIGHT DOWN through the center of the green light onto the building where Tiffany and the other alien lovers stood.

Around the world the same beam of light was brightening the skies. In Paris, it hit the top of Notre Dame Cathedral. In Tokyo it hit the Emperor's Palace. In Berlin it fell on the old Reichstag Building. It fell on the convention center in San Francisco and the Empire State Building in New York. It hit China's Great Wall and Tel Aviv's Great Synagogue, the statue of Nelson in London's Trafalgar Square, and in Washington, D.C., it fixed itself over the White House.

The light seemed to hold the whole world in a trance. No one was moving. Some people were paralyzed with fear and others were transfixed in awe. It was a global moment of silence.

Then the silence was over. The green beam became much brighter. It was much too bright to look at. Everyone within two miles turned away from it. They buried their faces in their arms. Then the noise started. It was like a roaring thunder that made the whole earth shake. People were grabbing their ears and shrieking in pain, but the horrible pounding thunder drowned out all other noise. Then, it stopped. For one moment, everyone thought that the worst was over.

Zam! A needle thin beam of white light shot out of the huge tower. All at once, the alien lovers' building exploded from the inside out. It shattered into a billion tiny pieces the size of postage stamps. Tiffany never had time to scream.

The thundering wave of light poured down with unbelievable force and within two seconds, a blast of fire flared up and began to roll forward. It spread in every direction at once and took out everything in its path. Cars were hurled into the air. Every tree and every street sign was blown apart. Even the asphalt on the street was ripped from the ground. Buildings fell apart like scarecrows caught in a tornado as the city was smothered under a thick layer of fire. The city of Los Angeles was being completely peeled away.

The horrible wave of fire moved over its path with slow determination. It gave its victims plenty of time to see it coming, but there was nothing they could do about it. There was no place to hide. Everyone turned and ran out of instinct, but there was no escape.

In Washington, D.C., the second helicopter was taking off from the White House lawn when the countdown ended. The blast of the beam started at the White House and moved its way outward in the form of fire. It shredded everything in its way, including the monuments, the museums, the Pentagon, and the little helicopter that never saw it coming.

The same nightmarish scene was repeating itself all over the globe. Thirty-six of the world's most beloved cities, along with all of their inhabitants, were completely destroyed.

The countdown on David's laptop had ticked down to 00:00 six seconds before the rear wheels of Air Force One lifted off the runway. An intense burst of light rushed through the plane as Washington was ruined. As the plane began to climb, everyone held their breath. Would they make it out alive? The heat from the wave of fire that was now rushing over the city violently shoved the plane through the air. It was like a giant hand was pitching them out of the capital city. Air Force One had escaped.

JASMINE WAS STILL JAMMED SMACK IN THE middle of the freeway tunnel when the beam hit downtown Los Angeles. The radio announcer said, "My God, it's destroying everything in its path. It's widening and—" The radio went dead.

Suddenly a light from behind Jas caught her eye. She looked in the rearview mirror and saw the wave of fire headed straight for them. Her instincts took over. She jumped out of the car and threw her bags on the ground. Boomer jumped out and Dylan jumped into her arms. Jasmine broke into a full sprint through the screaming people and stuck cars. As she looked over her shoulder, all she could see was the raging red and orange fire. She saw the door to a maintenance alcove coming up on her left. She ran to it and tried the handle, but it was jammed. Jasmine kicked the door as hard as she had ever kicked anything in her life.

Cars had been lifted in the air by the blaze and were sailing through the top of the tunnel. The door finally gave and she jumped inside with Dylan. She shielded her son from the blaze as best she could as she screamed at her sweet, dopey dog who was standing on a car roof a few feet away. *"BOOMER!"* she screamed as loud as she could. Boomer wagged his tail and took a huge jump to where she hid. As he did, the fire rushed through the rest of the tunnel and sent everything in its path crashing down.

Then, suddenly, it was over. Thousands of tons of boulders and loose earth clogged the tunnel at both ends. The entire hillside had collapsed. Jasmine rolled over onto her back and stared into the dark. She knew they were lucky to be alive. What she didn't know was that they were buried underneath a million pounds of dirt.

NO ONE WAS ALIVE IN THE WORLD'S THIRTY-six cities to see the giant tower retract back into the spaceship. The petal-shaped doors raised slowly to form an airtight seal. The city destroyers were ready to move on to their next set of targets.

"I'VE BEEN SAYIN' IT! I'VE BEEN SAYIN' IT FOR ten darn years. Haven't I been sayin' it, Miguel?" asked Russell as they cruised along in their beat-up home on wheels.

"Yeah, you've been sayin' it," Miguel said.

"Kids, haven't I been warnin' people? No one ever listened, but they'll be listenin' to Russell Casse from now on, boy," Russell said as he took a man-sized gulp of whiskey. He had no idea how upset his children were by what they were hearing on the radio. All he could think about was how people would finally stop laughing in his face when he mentioned his abduction.

A weak voice came from the back of the motor home, "You guys," said Troy, "I don't feel so good. Pull it over, I've gotta be sick."

"When's the last time you took your medicine Troy-boy?" asked Russell.

"I can't remember," the boy moaned. "I think about three or four days ago."

"What?" yelled Miguel. "But I just gave you some this morning!"

"Yeah, well, I didn't take it all right? I didn't think I needed it anymore. Now pull it over. I'm gonna puke."

Alicia helped her brother out of the car to some bushes.

Russell stumbled to the top of a hillside where he could get a view of the valley below.

"Miguel!" called Russell. "Come take a look at this!"

The valley was a sea of headlights. A thousand campers, motor homes, RVs, and passenger vehicles were on the move. In its own way, it was a beautiful sight.

"Ain't that something?" Russell asked.

"Maybe someone down there has some medicine for Troy," said Miguel. "Let's go find out."

STEVE SAT AT THE COUNTER IN THE BASE'S cafeteria and dialed Jasmine's phone number over and over. Every time a mechanical voice would come on saying that his call could not go through and to try again later. He would dial again.

Steve knew that his base commanders were ready to go after the beastly spaceships, but they were waiting for the go-ahead from Washington. In the meantime, Steve would keep dialing. His imagination began to eat at him. He was imagining all sorts of horrible things happening to Jasmine and Dylan.

"Let's roll, daddy-o," Jimmy shouted as he slid into the empty cafeteria. "Orders just came in." Jimmy was already in his flight suit and anxious to get in the face of the monsters in the sky. He noticed that Steve was upset. "What's up, man?"

"I can't get through to my parents' house, or to Jasmine. She was supposed to be here hours ago!"

Jimmy realized that he was going to have to be the one to give Steve some tough news. He spoke very carefully and put his hand on his buddy's shoulder. "Hey, brother, didn't you hear? These freakazoid spacemen took Los Angeles out. Blew it up. They did the same to New York and Washington, D.C. They're packing some very serious firepower, bro."

Steve suddenly felt like his head was going to explode. "No, Jimmy, that can't be! Why didn't I just put her in the car with me? This can't be happening . . ."

"Look man, Jas is a smart girl. I'm sure she got out of there all right," Jimmy said. "Now come on, there's a meeting in the briefing room in five minutes. Let's go."

Steve walked into the meeting ten minutes late. All thirty-five pilots of the Black Knights were sitting at school desks listening to Lieutenant Colonel Watson feed them information about the enemy. When Steve showed up late, the lieutenant colonel had to say something. Even a day as strange as today wasn't a good enough reason to break the rules.

"Captain Hiller! So nice of you to find time to join us!" he said.

Steve quickly found his seat next to Jimmy and listened to the briefing. Watson described how the huge mother ship was hiding itself behind the moon, and how the city destroyer ships had fallen away from its base and settled over thirty-six cities around the world. Thirty-six cities that no longer existed. They passed around a grainy satellite photo of the huge helmet-shaped mother ship.

Steve could tell that everyone was looking at him to see if he was okay. Jimmy had obviously told them how upset he was. He was their leader in the air, and they had to know that he was in control before they followed him. Steve was a true professional, though. He wanted nothing more than to get in his plane and lead an attack on these deadly ships. As Gamont continued to lecture, Steve leaned over to Jimmy and whispered, "You scared, man?"

"Nope. You?" asked Jimmy.

"Naw," Steve said, but then pretended like he was about to cry. "Actually, I am! Hold me, Jimmy!" That was it. The Black Knights erupted in laughter.

Normally Lieutenant Colonel Watson would have been angry, but he knew that Steve was showing everyone that he was fine. He still had to say something to Steve for interrupting, though.

"Something you'd like to add to the briefing, Captain Hiller?" he asked.

"No, sir. I'm just real anxious to go up there and whup ET's butt."

"You'll get your chance," said the commanding officer.

THE BLACK KNIGHTS WALKED WITH confidence out to their waiting F/A–18 fighter jets. As they approached the hangar, the huge doors rolled open. Technicians were milling about making last-minute adjustments. Steve decided it was time to give his men a little pep talk.

"Now remember, we're the first ones up there, so we're just gonna go check them out. If we run into anything really hairy, we get away fast, got it? We're the best there is, men, let's go prove it."

As they walked to their planes. Steve yelled over his shoulder, "Hey, Jimmy, you got our Victory Dance?"

"Yessir, Captain, got it right here," said Jimmy as he produced two cigars from his breast pocket. He stuck one in his mouth and bit off the end.

"Yo, we don't light up till we win, bro! Not till the fat lady sings, got it?" asked Steve.

"Aye aye, Captain, I got it," said Jimmy.

As soon as Steve was alone in his plane, he doubled over in pain. He couldn't stop thinking about Jasmine and Dylan. The pilots ran through a quick equipment check and fired up their engines.

THE PRESIDENT SAT BY HIMSELF STARING out the window. Constance slipped into one of the big leather chairs next to him. Everyone on the plane was suffering through their own personal state of shock, but for the president, it was much worse. Millions of Americans had died in the last hour and he felt responsible.

"How could you have known, Tom? Stop blaming yourself," Connie said.

President Whitmore couldn't look at her. He

continued to stare out the window and said, "I could have evacuated the cities hours ago. I should have. A lot of people died today, Connie. How many of them didn't have to?"

She realized there was nothing she could say to make him feel any better. She sat by his side in silent support. General Grey came down the aisle and took a seat beside them both. President Whitmore looked up. "Any news of my wife?"

General Grey's face was even more serious than usual. "The helicopter hasn't arrived and there has been no radio contact. I'm very sorry, Tom."

The president's face was drained of all its color. He felt like he'd just been kicked in the gut. He tried to regain his presidential air. "What other news have you got?"

"The fighters are in the air," said General Grey.

President Whitmore rose to his feet and walked to the back of the plane. He now knew exactly what had to be done. It was time to make war.

A little control room on Air Force One had been set up as the military command center. It was jammed full of high-tech equipment that buzzed and rattled as it turned out information on the exact location of the Black Knights. Technicians wearing headphones worked at computers as they received new information about the movement of the city destroyers.

General Grey moved to where the president was standing and reported on his latest information. "All satellite, microwave, and ground communications with the target cities are gone, Mr. President. We believe we're looking at a total loss."

The president looked up at one of the tracking screens.

"Where are the fighters?" he asked.

"Estimated contact with target is four minutes, sir," a technician reported.

Out in the passenger area, David was wearing a barf bag like it was a feed sack. He was not a big fan of flying.

"It's Air Force One, for crying out loud!" said Julius. "Still, you get sick!"

"Dad, please," David was holding back another wave of nausea. "Don't speak."

Telling Julius not to speak only got him talking faster. "Look at me," said Julius as he gave himself a good whack in the tummy, "I'm solid as a rock. It could be good weather, bad weather, it doesn't matter." David was two shades of green, but Julius continued, illustrating with his hands. "We could go up down, back forth, side to side . . . "

David made a run for the bathroom. Julius looked at Connie and asked, "What'd I say?"

Connie slid into the seat next to her father-in-law. "He still gets air sick, huh?" Connie turned in her chair to face Julius. "Listen, in all of this craziness, I didn't get a chance to thank you two."

"Think nothing of it, Spanky," said Julius.

"Spunky." Constance smiled. "He told you that, huh?"

"You know, all he could do was think about getting to you. There's still love there, I think," Julius said.

"Love was never our problem," she said sadly.

"'All you need is love,' said John Lennon." Julius was trying to be philosophical. "Smart man. Shot in the back. Very sad."

Connie couldn't quite figure out the point the old man was trying to make, but she knew he meant well. She smiled and nodded.

JASMINE HAD BEEN WALKING AROUND IN dark tunnels for hours, looking for an exit. The damp walls were full of slimy surprises. The three walked on and on until they heard water trickling far away. She walked toward the sound and suddenly felt a slight breeze coming from up ahead. She found a small opening where light from outside was getting in. Jasmine pulled a grate off the hole and pulled herself through. "I think we found a way out, baby," she said to Dylan, who was trying to be very brave.

A few minutes later, the three of them were walking toward the sunlight at the open mouth of an upper tunnel. An overturned car was smoldering just outside. Everywhere they looked, their city was destroyed. All of the concrete and asphalt that made up the streets and sidewalks was now just a heap of rocks. Most buildings were completely gone. Some were still half-standing, with small fires burning on top. There was no sign of life anywhere, and for a moment Jasmine wondered if she and Dylan were the last people on earth.

Dylan began to cry. "Mommy, what happened?"

"I don't know, baby."

High above them the roar of jet fighters filled the sky. They were headed for the spaceship.

"Is that Steve in those planes?" asked Dylan.

"It might be," said Jasmine. "Why don't you wave just in case."

THE BLACK KNIGHTS WERE MINUTES AWAY from their destination. The spaceship was visible on the horizon, hanging like a cruel joke over the devastated countryside. Steve couldn't believe his eyes when he saw the destruction below him. Jasmine must be dead, he thought. He punched the wall of his cockpit.

"Don't sweat it, daddy-o," Jimmy said over the radio to Steve. "I'm sure she made it out in time." The line stayed quiet for a long time until Steve spoke to the entire squad.

"Here we go, boys. Time to lock and load."

Then Air Force One took over the airwaves. General Grey addressed the men. "Gentlemen this is Air Force General Grey speaking, Chief Commander of Allied Space Command. On behalf of the president of the United States, I want to wish you all a successful mission. You may fire at will."

The pilots each prepared to launch their first missiles. They dropped away and sped after the target. It looked like a flea circus rushing toward a Mack truck. The Knights began to pull up. They knew it would take several hits to bring down a ship this big. They kept a careful eye on their missiles. Suddenly, when the missiles were still a quarter of a mile away from their target, they all exploded at the same time.

"I didn't even see them fire!" Jimmy yelled.

"All right, men," said Steve, "let's switch to Sidewinders."

General Grey came back on. "Good call, Knight One. Spread formation."

Sidewinder missiles had to be fired at a closer range, but they were a tougher test of the spaceship's air-to-air defense capabilities. Instead of thirty bombs, this time the aliens would have eighty to shoot at.

"Everyone check your radar. Let's launch at one mile," said Steve.

Steve knew that one mile was cutting it pretty close when they were flying at four hundred miles an hour, but he really wanted to do some damage this time.

"Attack!"

Six missiles fired from each fighter. All at once, when they reached the same quarter mile from the spaceship, the missiles exploded.

"Pull up! Pull up!" Steve screamed. "They've got a shield!" Steve threw his plane straight up and twenty-nine of the men followed. The last pilot came in too fast. His jet did a belly flop against the invisible force field.

"Let's head home," said Steve. There was no use trying to take out the ship this way. It wasn't doing any good.

But it was too late to get away unnoticed. A set of massive doors was opening and out flew a storm of attacker planes. Fifty gray ships that looked like sharks' fins were headed straight for the Black Knights.

The attackers began to pick off the Knights immediately. They fought back, but the fighter planes from another world didn't seem to sustain any kind of damage no matter what the Knights did. When seen from a distance, the attacker ships looked like a swarm of bats.

"Mayday! Mayday!" yelled Steve. They were now surrounded by the faster enemy planes. One of them sat right on Steve's tail.

"Evasive maneuvers!" he commanded as he threw his own plane into a sideways loop. He narrowly missed a storm of lasers from the enemy attacker. All around him, his men were being blown away.

On Air Force One, the men in the control room could hear the casualties that the Black Knights were receiving.

"Get them out of there!" yelled President Whitmore.

"I've got you covered, Stevie," said Jimmy from behind him. Jimmy fired another Sidewinder at the attacker, but five yards before it reached the ship, the missile exploded. "They got shields, too!" Jimmy yelled.

Suddenly, Jimmy was being trailed by two of the attackers. Steve saw what was happening. "Jimmy, roll right. I'll cover." Jimmy narrowly avoided a shower of laser fire. The sky was now littered with the fiery wreckage of America's elite air strike force.

"Let's outrun 'em. Follow my lead," Steve said to Jimmy. They both threw their F/A–18s into high gear and sped east as fast as they could go, but the alien attackers kept up with them. They were going so fast, it was difficult to not feel sick. The attackers were gaining on them.

"Jimmy, kick it! They're gaining on us," said Steve.

"I can't go any faster, man," Jimmy said. He was beginning to lose consciousness. His plane started to climb.

"Keep it straight, Jimmy. Stay with me," Steve yelled at him.

"I can't man, I'm sorry."

"Don't wimp out on me, Jimmy! We're in this together. All the way, bro!"

"Stevie . . . I can't . . . " Jimmy ripped off his oxygen mask and started to gasp for air.

"Put your mask back on Jimmy! That's an order, Marine!"

But Jimmy was out cold. His plane began to drift off to the right, and an alien attacker jumped on his tail. Laser fire showered Jimmy's jet and it exploded.

"No! No! Jimmy!" Steve couldn't believe what he had just seen. He threw his plane into even higher gear and screamed at the top of his lungs. At that moment, he would have flown his jet straight into any attacker that got in his way.

Steve quickly tried to get himself back together and figure a way out of this mess. There was a single attacker gaining on him from behind. "Okay, you little weasel, let's see how good you really are." Steve headed straight for the Grand Canyon.

Steve cut his engines without warning. The attacker was surprised and sailed past as he dove into the canyon. The attacker followed him down and caught up in no time.

"All right, now, let's see who's the man." Steve began to try every trick he had ever learned. He was swerving, banking, and diving all over the place. The attacker followed him as best it could. Occasionally, it would scrape along the canyon wall, but due to its protective shield, it didn't receive any damage.

The attacker was keeping up with Steve so well that it even managed to get a few shots off. Steve was feeling the pressure and ducked into a much smaller side canyon. Inside these narrow walls, there was no room for error. He was just waiting for the clumsy attacker to plow into the rocks. But before Steve could go any further with his plan, the low-fuel light began to flash on his instrument panel. He couldn't believe his bad luck.

"You are really starting to burn me up, you Darth Vader wannabe!" he yelled.

Then, a plan came to him. Not far ahead, the canyon came to a dead end. He eased off his speed and hit the "Fuel Drop" button. Reserve fuel in both tanks spewed into the air behind him and splattered the attacker. He hit his afterburners to ignite the fuel in the air and created a trail of fire behind him. Steve laughed an evil laugh of victory until he looked behind him. The attacker burst through the flames without a scratch.

"Okay, Plan B, you little cretin," said Steve. "Let's see if you can fly undercover." With that Steve launched the plane's drag parachute out of the back of his fighter. The chute opened wide into the air and the attacker flew right into it. Steve knew it was only a matter of seconds before he would get rear-ended, so he tightened up his seat belt and pointed his jet straight at the canyon wall. Two hundred feet from impact, Steve shut his eyes and yanked up hard on the ejection lever. His entire seat sprang out of the plane. A second later, his jet plowed into the canyon wall with a huge *KABOOM!*

The alien pilot had lost the parachute that had

been covering its windshield, and now it could see the wall in front of it. The attacker pulled up at the last second and made a crash landing onto the desert floor.

Captain Hiller laughed as loud as he could at the broken attacker. He floated down through the hot Arizona morning to a hard landing a couple of hundred yards away. He was a bit dizzy from the whole experience, but his blood was still boiling. He quickly freed himself from his chair and chute and marched toward the smoking ship.

The attacker was an amazing sight to see up close. It was protected by a dozen plates of armor that almost looked alive. The entire structure looked more like a plant or animal, not a machine. It was oozing some sort of clear gooey fluid. Steve took a few careful steps, but the shield was down. He took seven giant steps to get to the center of the craft and yanked the door open.

As quickly as the door opened, out popped a living creature, an alien. Its squirming tentacles were flying everywhere and its large shell-like head thrust itself out into the sunlight. Its eyes were cold black like an insect's. A thick bony neck came to a point at the top of its head and a deep gash ran right up the center of the face.

Steve was repulsed by the look of the thing. On impulse, he pulled his arm back and punched it square in the face. The monster's bony head bounced off the side of the ship and it collapsed.

"Welcome to earth," Steve said.

Steve turned around and sat down. He had just realized how exhausted he was. He took a deep breath and pulled out his Victory Dance cigar that he had planned to enjoy with Jimmy.

"Now that's what I call a close encounter," he said to himself.

HUNDREDS OF PEOPLE IN MOTOR HOMES had gathered together in Death Valley. People were milling about everywhere trying to figure out their next move. Russell had assumed a leadership role in the group. He had managed to not tell anyone about his abduction, and he was helping the others in his group stay focused on making plans. They decided to head for Las Vegas for gas and supplies and then head for the wide-open desert of Arizona.

Troy was getting worse. Miguel had been walking around the camp for hours looking for some medicine for his brother. No one seemed to have anything that would help. Troy was lying in the back of the motor home under a thick pile of blankets. Russell sat next to him with a cold compress while Alicia made him more tea.

"You know," said Russell in a soft voice, "you're just like your mother used to be. I had to twist her arm to get her to take her medicine."

"I'm not going to die like Mom, am I, Dad?" asked Troy.

"No, no," said Russell.

Alicia stepped into the back room. "You're going to be fine."

Miguel joined his family by the bed. "I couldn't find anything. Someone said there's a spaceship headed this way. Everyone's moving out."

"Then we better get a move on," said Russell. "Let's head for Vegas. We're sure to find you some medicine, Troy."

There was a knock at the motor home door. Alicia went to answer. On the other side of the screen was a handsome young boy, about her age, with curly blond hair. The two had met a few hours earlier after several shy smiles across the campsite. His name was Philip and he had said he might know someone who had some medicine. He stood there with penicillin in hand.

"Here, I found this," he handed it to her. "It should help keep his fever down."

"It's really nice of you to help us," Alicia said.

Russell came to the door to check the boy out. He scowled at him and Philip took a few steps back.

"I wish I could do more," Philip said, "but we're heading out."

"I'm going with you!" Alicia blurted out. Then she turned bright red. She couldn't believe she just said that. "I mean, we're going, too."

Russell had had enough of the young pups flirting. "Tell that punk to shut the door and get out of here. Go sniff around somewhere else."

Alicia was so embarrassed she wanted to dive into a hole and never come out. Through her teeth, she begged, "Dad!"

Philip smiled at her to try and make her feel better. "Well, see you round."

"Okay . . . " Alicia was in heaven, ". . . bye."

When she shut the door, all of the Casse men were giving her a suspicious look. "What? I was only being nice because he gave us some medicine."

"Yeah, right," they all said.

ABOARD AIR FORCE ONE, GENERAL GREY and President Whitmore were able to monitor all ground bases. The information was pretty grim. Not only had their F/A–18s suffered a tough defeat in the air, the country's ground resources were being devastated by the enemies. The last thing Air Force One heard from El Toro was, "Incoming! Hostile incoming!" Before a single plane could get off the ground, the base had become a smoldering pile of rubble.

"This is unbelievable," the president said to General Grey, "not only do they know how to hit us, they know exactly where and in what order."

"Yes, sir," said General Grey, "it's an extremely well-planned attack. They seem to fully understand our defense system."

David was helping himself back to his seat little by little. He was still pretty queasy. As he took a breather against the cabin wall, he overheard the conversation that Secretary Nimziki had started. He was informing the president that the logical next course of action would be to launch a full-scale nuclear attack. The president, however, wasn't agreeable to his suggestion. "Above American soil? Do you know what you're saying? We would be killing tens of thousands of innocent civilians."

Nimziki had predicted that the president wouldn't go for the idea. He decided to try and make him look weak in front of everyone. " If we don't strike soon, there may not be much of an America left to defend. A delay now would be even more costly than when you waited to evacuate the cities!"

Before the argument got any more heated, an officer stepped in the room to address General Grey.

"Any word from NORAD?" General Grey asked.

"It's gone, sir. They've taken it out," the officer said.

"That's impossible!" said General Grey. NORAD was buried deep within a mountain in Colorado and was supposed to be the most secure place in the world. Even if every city in the United States was wiped out, the technicians at NORAD would still be able to track enemy movement. The president's cabinet had been sent there hours ago. General Grey kept shaking his head in disbelief. "The vice president, the joint chiefs . . . " It was shocking news. They would have to find someplace else to land.

Secretary Nimziki spoke again, only this time the president was listening. "Mr. President, the time for a nuclear attack is now."

Upon hearing these words, David could no longer stand by outside the door. He knew it wasn't his place to barge into their room, but they were about to commit the biggest crime yet, in David's mind.

"You're not serious!" David yelled as he entered. "You're going to fire nuclear weapons over your own people?"

Connie walked straight toward David to push him out and calm him down. David was a very calm, mild-mannered person until he got angry like he was now, and then, watch out.

"If you start firing nukes, then everyone's gonna be firing them! Do you have any idea what that kind of fallout is going to do to the planet? Have you—" David was cut off.

"Shut up! Get him out of here!" Nimziki had lost all patience with this man.

"Don't you tell him to shut up!" said Julius as he joined the commotion. "You'd all be dead if it weren't for my David!" Julius shook his finger in Nimziki's face. "I blame all of you for what's happening. You knew this was going to happen and you did nothing!"

The president took a deep breath and regained his calm. "Sir, this caught us totally unprepared. We're as surprised as anyone."

"Don't give me that! Since the fifties you've had

that spaceship that you took out of the desert—"
Julius started.

"Dad, please." David was beginning to get embarrassed. His father watched way too much TV.

"What was it called . . . *Roswell!* That's it. You had the spaceship and the alien bodies locked up in that secret place, Area Fifty-One, that's it! You knew all this time and you did nothing!"

President Whitmore was amused by the old man's accusation. Over his career, Area 51 had come up many times. It made him laugh to think that some people thought the government had so many dark secrets.

"Regardless of what you've read in magazines, there have never been any spaceships recovered by the government."

Secretary Nimziki cleared his throat. Everyone turned to stare at him. "Excuse me, Mr. President—" he cleared his throat again, "—that's not entirely accurate."

The room was silent as Nimziki explained that Area 51, a secret military base in the Nevada desert, did house a spaceship. And a few aliens, too.

The president could hardly take another surprise today. He sat down and ran his hands through his hair.

"Take me to it."

JASMINE, DYLAN, AND BOOMER CONTINUED to walk through the smoldering cinders that used to be

Los Angeles. It was difficult to recognize anything, but Jasmine knew she had better find something to eat and somewhere to sleep for her son.

She hurried down a slope to where she could see an old red truck stored in a parking garage. It looked like it was in amazingly good condition. Jasmine climbed up into the cab and rustled around for the keys. They fell from the sun visor above her. "Yes! Come on, Dylan! Boomer! Hop in!" She started to rev the engine. *Maybe now, at last,* she thought, *I can get to El Toro.*

Jasmine plowed down the road where the street used to be. Occasionally, she would see someone lying or standing in the rubble and pick them up. They would climb into the back of the truck along with the other survivors. Some were bleeding and some were sobbing. Others were just sitting quietly and staring off into space in absolute shock.

Jasmine was choosing the direction to drive based on the placement of the sun. She thought she had figured out which way south was and was heading that way now. She knew that all of the people in the back of the truck could receive medical care at the base's hospital.

As she cruised along, Jasmine suddenly saw a very thin man standing on the top of a huge pile of rubble. He was holding up a cross and yelling.

"Repent sinners! He speaketh his word and the end hath come!"

"Yo!" Jasmine yelled, stopping the truck briefly. "We're headed for El Toro. Hop on!"

"You cannot go against the word, sister. The end hath come!"

"Well, whatever," Jasmine said to herself. She had no time to cure the crazy. She kicked the truck back into gear and took off.

A little further down the road, she spotted a smoking helicopter and what looked like a couple of bodies lying next to it. She stopped the truck and ran up to it. Boomer and Dylan followed. As they got closer to the crash site, Jasmine realized that the woman lying beside the ruins of the helicopter was the First Lady of the United States, Marilyn Whitmore. Mrs. Whitmore was attempting to lift the metal door from the helicopter that lay on top of her. The pilot and Secret Service agent who lay beside her were both dead. Jasmine ran over to help her.

"Hey, stay still now!" Jasmine motioned to one of the men in the truck to help her. "We'll get you to a hospital right away."

Just then, a rifle cocked. Jasmine spun around to see a beer-bellied man with a hunting jacket walking up to her. Two more men followed behind. The leader was practically drooling as he stared at Jasmine's truck keys.

"Looks like I've solved our transportation problem," the man said to his friends. He smiled a toothless grin at Jasmine. "Now, why don't you hand over those keys, witch?"

This was the last thing Jasmine needed. She tried

to be pleasant while she shielded Dylan's body with her own. "We were just leaving here, anyway. You're welcome to come with us."

"I don't think so. Now give me the keys or I'll shoot your dog." The man pointed his gun straight at Boomer.

At that moment, the crazy preacher-man showed up. "Repent sinners! The end hath come!"

"This ain't yer business," said the man. "Get outta here, wacko!"

While the men were talking back and forth, Jasmine noticed the fireworks that Steve had given Dylan sticking out of the top of his backpack. She shielded the wicks with her hand, and quickly tried to light one.

"You cannot go against the word, brother!" shouted the crazy man.

"Sure I can," said the man with the gun. He fired one shot and struck the preacher man down.

Now he turned his attention back to Jasmine. "Now give me that key, witch."

With the wick ignited, Jasmine quickly turned to face the man and shot the bottle rocket straight at him. It hit him squarely in the chest and lit his shirt on fire. He dropped the rifle to put out the flames. Jasmine dove for the gun.

"This witch was born in Alabama with a daddy who loved to hunt," Jasmine said as she cocked the rifle and pointed it at the scared men, "so don't think for one second that I don't know how to use this." She fired one shot into the air and the men ran for the hills.

Jasmine carried Mrs. Whitmore to the back of the truck and carefully laid her down. The First Lady could barely move, but she opened her mouth slightly to whisper, "That was brave."

STEVE FELT LIKE HE WAS ABOUT TO MELT into a pool of sweat. He tried switching shoulders to give himself a rest, but it didn't do much good. He had wrapped the big alien in his parachute and was dragging it across the desert. *Any minute now,* Steve kept thinking, *someone is going to find me and take this thing off of my hands.* But in the meantime, it was all his.

"Ya know," Steve said to the still unconscious alien, "this was supposed to be my weekend off. But nooo! You've got me pullin' your potato-chip-eating, slime-dripping butt across the burning desert with your dreadlocks hangin' out the back of my parachute." The creature's long tentacles were dragging limply behind. He stopped for a second and made a sour face. "And what the heck is that smell?" Steve dropped the parachute strap and let his anger loose again. He kicked at the alien and yelled, "I should have been at a barbecue!" After a minute, he had to stop to catch his breath. As he stood there panting, he thought he heard the faint rumble of a car engine. He looked up to see an amazing sight on the horizon: motor homes. Hundreds of them.

It was an enormous troop of vehicles of all kinds, led by Russell Casse. Russell spotted the man with the parachute waving his arms in the air and slowed to a stop. The rest of the vehicles followed.

"Need a ride, soldier?" Russell asked sarcastically.

"When I flew overhead, I saw a base not too far from here," Steve said.

Russell consulted his AAA Travel Guide. "It ain't on the map."

"Trust me, it's there," said Steve.

"Maybe we can get medicine there," offered Miguel.

No one in the motor home group was exactly excited about having an alien with them, but Russell felt like somehow his abduction experience was coming full circle. Maybe running into this young marine who was dragging one of the creatures through the middle of the desert was some kind of sign. Maybe it was a reminder of what he had to do.

They turned themselves east and headed for the base that Steve claimed to have seen.

FROM THE SKY, AREA 51 HARDLY LOOKED like a top secret anything. Instead it looked like a shabby, beat-up little airport that had been abandoned many years before. As the president stared down at the place, he had a hard time believing it held a spaceship.

Air Force One touched down, and everyone crowded the doorway to be let out. As they flew through the sky hearing about destruction after destruction, some of the passengers aboard wondered if their feet would ever touch land again. But here they were, and it felt really good.

Large hangar doors rolled open and the base's top administrator, Major Mitchell, walked out to greet the visitors. He was a tall, handsome man and a perfect example of military excellence. His voice was full of authority.

"Welcome to Area Fifty-One, sir," he said with a crisp salute to the president.

"We're in a hurry," the president said, returning the salute.

"Right this way, sir," said Mitchell as he led the group into the mysterious buildings below. He led them into a dead-end hallway and instructed everyone to watch their backs. He flipped a switch and the room began to descend, deep into the ground. As they sank into the high-tech vault of government secrets, the president was growing angrier and angrier. He glared at Nimziki.

"Why wasn't I told about this place?" he asked.

"Two words, Mr. President: plausible deniability," Nimziki said. "If news of Area Fifty-

One was ever leaked to the public, it would be crucial for America to believe that you didn't know about it." For Nimziki, this explained everything. For President Whitmore, this explanation only made his blood boil even more.

As the elevator came to a rest, the metal doors slid open and revealed what looked like a research hospital. Behind two enormous glass doors, scientists milled about everywhere in white suits, gloves, and masks. They were poking and prodding a few large gray objects that had intricate designs on them. The scientists stopped their work and stared at the arriving visitors.

"Let's have a look," said President Whitmore.

"I'm sorry sir, this is a static-free clean room, we can't enter—"

"Open the door," the president interrupted.

"Yes, sir," said Major Mitchell. He slid his magnetized ID badge through the scanner lock and the doors slid open. The group of eleven amazed visitors walked down the runway in the middle of the room. Despite his anger, President Whitmore couldn't help but be impressed with the operation he saw around him. In every detail, the lab was well staffed, well supplied, and well organized.

A man in a long white coat approached the group from the end of the hall. He had long, scraggly gray hair and wore glasses that hadn't been popular since the early sixties. He was smiling from ear to ear and staring right at the president. At forty-five years old, he was an overgrown nerd. He was followed by another scientist in a lab coat.

"Mr. President, wow," the man said. He extended his hand, "I'm Dr. Okun. I head up all research here at Area Fifty-One."

The other scientist chimed in. "I'm Dr. Isaacs." He shook the president's hand with great enthusiasm and smiled like an idiot.

Dr. Okun realized that they had overdone it. "Sorry," he said, "they don't let us out much."

President Whitmore gave him a good looking over and nodded. "Yes, I can understand that."

"So," Dr. Okun clapped his hands together, "you guys wanna see the big tamale?"

Everyone looked at one another and nodded. Whatever the big tamale was, they were ready to see it. They walked down to the end of the facility and Dr. Okun pushed the release button that slowly lowered the hatch. It opened like an upside-down garage door. Slowly, starting at the top, the group got their first glimpse of the spaceship that the government had recovered in New Mexico in the 1950s. It looked identical to the one that had been chasing Steve through the Grand Canyon.

The chamber that held the ship was five stories tall and five stories wide.

The ship inside seemed to be glowing a dark, midnight blue from the dim lights surrounding it.

The ship was unlike anything that any of them had ever seen before. They all stood motionless with their mouths wide open. Facing the front of the tower was a cockpit with wide, flat windows. At the nose of the ship, curved objects came forward to form a sharp projection. Scientists and technicians moved all around the ship making minor adjustments and scanning the surface with strange blue lamps.

"Ain't she a beaut?" Dr. Okun asked, like the proud owner of a race horse.

Julius couldn't resist getting his two cents in. "Ha! Never any spaceships recovered by the government, huh?"

"All of these designs," said President Whitmore as he scanned over the surface of the ship, "what do they mean?"

"Who knows?" said Okun, as if he'd never thought of the question. Actually, he'd been thinking about that very question for months on end.

"Are you telling me we've had one of their ships here for forty years and we don't know anything about them?" Whitmore snapped.

"Oh, no, no! We know tons about them," Okun said. "But the supercool stuff only started when the other guys showed up. The last forty-eight hours have been really exciting."

The president exploded. "Millions of people are dying out there. I don't think 'exciting' is the word I'd choose to describe it." His words echoed through the huge room. He couldn't stop thinking about Marilyn, but he didn't want the others to see him crack. He rubbed his temples, as if he had a headache, to hide the tears that were coming to his eyes.

"Dr. Okun, can you tell us anything that would be useful?" General Grey asked.

"Well, let's see," said Dr. Okun, "They're very similar to us in a lot of ways. They breathe oxygen and have similar tolerances to heat and cold. That's probably why they're interested in our planet."

"Why do you think they're interested in our planet?" asked David.

"It's just a hunch of mine," Dr. Okun said. "They're animals just like us, with a survival instinct. Maybe something happened on their last planet to drive them away. Now they need a new home." Suddenly a huge smile spread across the doctor's face. "Hey, you guys want to see them?"

"Let's go," said President Whitmore.

THE CONTAINMENT LABORATORY WHERE THE aliens were kept looked like a top secret safe in a high-security bank. Dr. Okun typed in a security code and the huge, thick door unlocked. They walked into the dark chamber where they could faintly see the outlines of three large cylinders in front of them.

"This, ladies and gentlemen, is what we call 'The Freak Show.'" Dr. Okun giggled. No one else was enjoying his humor, though, so he cleared his throat and turned up the lights.

The cylinders began to lift upward, and inside were three glass tanks. Each one contained the body of a dead alien. Their skin was a pale peach color and was so transparent, every vein, artery and organ was visible. Their oversized, vase-shaped heads held their pure black, almond-shaped eyes. Even though they were very dead, their eyes still gave them an evil gaze.

"When these three were found, they were wearing some kind of suit of armor. We think maybe it was the body of another animal that they breed for the use of their bodies. The suits made them stand about eleven feet tall and they had tentacles. Really nasty-looking things. These little guys crawl right up inside and burrow into it like a cocoon. It's disgusting, really," said Dr. Okun.

No one else was talking. They all just stared in awe at the gruesome sight.

Dr. Okun continued. "Once we got their suits off, we were able to learn a great deal about them. They have no vocal chords, so we assume that they communicate through some other means."

This sparked David's curiosity. "What other means? You don't mean hand signals or sign language, do you?"

"No," Okun said, "we're thinking some kind of extrasensory perception."

"Telepathy," added Dr. Isaacs, "they read each others' minds."

President Whitmore stepped closer to one of the floating aliens. "Can they be killed?"

"These three died in the crash," said Dr. Okun. "Their bodies seem to be as delicate as our own. You just have to get past their technology, which is, I'm sorry to say, far more advanced than ours."

"David, you unlocked that technology," the president said. "You cracked their code."

"Oh, I don't know about that," David said. "All I did was stumble onto their signal. I don't know how helpful I can be."

"Show them what you've discovered," said the president. "Put your heads together and see if together you can come up with some answers." He then added, with a bit of a challenge, "Let's see if you're as smart as we all hope you are."

David stared at Whitmore over his glasses.

AS THE LONG LINE OF MOTOR HOMES reached the edge of where Steve had seen the base, they began to see signs everywhere that warned, "NO TRESPASSING," "GOVERNMENT PROPERTY," and "UNAUTHORIZED VISITORS SUBJECT TO IMMEDIATE ARREST."

Steve was riding in the back of a pickup truck with his captured visitor when they arrived at a guard post.

Two military men with guns walked out to stop the enormous line of vehicles. They rolled to a stop and Steve's truck cruised to the front to address the men.

One of the guards spoke up. "I'm sorry, Captain, this is a restricted area. I can't let you pass without clearance."

"Clearance? You're asking me for clearance?" After all that the world had been through in the last forty-eight hours, Steve couldn't believe that this man was acting as though it was still business as usual.

"Come here," Steve said to the guard. The guard looked confused. "It's all right, come here." The guard walked over to the truck and saw the parachute draped over something in the truck. Steve pulled back the cover and the guard jumped three feet in the air at the horrifying sight. "How about if I just leave this here with you?"

"Let him pass!" the guard shouted.

DAVID STOOD IN THE DARK WITH DR. OKUN inside the attacker ship. The front chamber was like nothing he had ever seen before. Even though it was metallic looking, it was also somehow living. The walls almost seemed to be breathing, and they were oozing a clear, thick goo. Dr. Okun was obviously excited to show the craft off to someone new.

"This is so supremely cool, don't you think?" he asked David as he pointed around the ship.

They moved to the cockpit, where the dashboard was full of buttons and furiously blinking lights.

"We've had people working around the clock," Dr. Okun said, "trying to get a fix on what all of this stuff does. Some of it, we've figured out. Like that clump of stuff over there. It seems to be a life-support system for the whole vehicle. And this," he pointed to a large flap at the bottom of the dashboard, "appears to be an accelerator pedal."

David sat down in one of the leather chairs. "These aren't the original seats, are they?"

"No. We replaced them so we would have someplace to sit while we studied. The seats they had were like huge gooey body pods." Okun continued, "We're pretty sure that these gizmos here," he pointed to another area, "are what they used to guide the craft."

"Can someone grab my laptop for me?" David asked the scientists standing outside.

"Find something interesting?" the doctor asked.

"Maybe," David said. After a technician retrieved his computer for him, he flipped it on and began to type. There was something very familiar about the green light on the attack ship's screen, something similar to the signal he had found. He pointed at the dashboard to explain his theory to Dr. Okun.

"These patterns on here," he pointed to a little screen on the dash, "they're repeating sequentially, just like the countdown signal." He turned his laptop to the doctor to show him the same pattern on its screen. "See. This is how they're coordinating their ships."

"You know," Dr. Okun said, staring at David, "you're really starting to make us look bad." The two men smiled at one another.

A technician ran into the hangar and shouted to everyone, "They got one! Someone just brought in a live one!"

THERE WAS A MASS COMMOTION OUTSIDE OF the hangar when the fleet of vehicles pulled up. One of the technicians inside immediately wheeled out a stretcher for the captured alien. Captain Hiller stayed close by its side. He wasn't about to give up his catch that easily. The hundreds of motorists were jumping out of their cars, trucks, and vans and asking to come inside. Major Mitchell came outside and took command of the situation. He grabbed a bullhorn and asked everyone to stay back.

Dr. Okun and Dr. Isaacs shoved their way through the crowd to get a look at the alien.

"How long has it been unconscious?" Dr. Okun asked Steve.

"About three hours," Steve said. He wasn't about to tell anyone how it got that way.

"Excuse me, doctor?" Russell pushed his way to the front. Dr. Okun ignored him.

"Get it into containment, stat," Dr. Okun ordered his assistants.

"Doctor, my boy is very sick. He has a problem with his adrenal cortex. We need help right away!" Russell was shouting, but it was no use—everyone was completely focused on the unconscious alien.

"He's drying out. Let's have some saline solution available immediately," said Dr. Isaacs. He pushed the button to get the elevator. But before the door could open, Russell grabbed Dr. Isaacs by his lab coat and slammed him against the wall. "If you don't help my son, he's going to die!" he yelled into the doctor's face.

Miguel, for once, was proud of his father. He had been standing in the middle of the crowd and watched the whole incident.

"Okay, listen," Dr. Isaacs was speaking slowly to calm the big man down, "O'Haver, Miller, come with me. Take us to him, all right?" Russell took his hands off the doctor and led them through the crowd to Troy.

JASMINE WAS STILL DETERMINED TO GET TO El Toro. She had her heart set that Steve would be there waiting for her. She had found that the freeway leading south was still okay, but she was taking the drive very slowly. After all, she had the injured First Lady riding in the back. When she got off the freeway at the El Toro exit, her heart began to sink. She looked around at the smoldering rubble on both sides of the road.

Jasmine pulled up to a locked gate that now protected nothing. She jumped out of the cab and walked toward it just to make sure her eyes weren't lying. A sign that read "WELCOME TO EL TORO MARINE CORPS AIR STATION" was still smoking on the side of the road. El Toro was gone. She buried her head in her arm and allowed herself to cry.

AS SOON AS GENERAL GREY HAD ARRIVED AT Area 51, he had quickly established a command center. The control room here was normally used to test experimental aircraft. It was well stocked with high-tech equipment and radar tracking screens, but almost none of it was working. The earth's communication networks had all been torn apart, and the situation was getting worse by the hour. The second wave of cities had all been destroyed, and now the ships were moving on to their next set of targets. Even here, deep underground and hundreds of miles from the nearest city destroyer, people were beginning to feel like the battle was hopeless. They knew that they were completely at the mercy of the creatures in the huge ships.

Technicians were frantically working all around the room, trying to get their communications equipment to respond. Secretary Nimziki walked into the room to try one of the phones.

"So, Nimziki, got any more tricks up your sleeve that might help us win this fight?" asked General Grey.

"That's a cheap shot, General. I was under direct orders to keep this place a secret, no matter what."

"Why didn't you say something when they first arrived? How many lives did we lose so you could keep your secret?"

"Hey, don't lay that guilt at my doorstep. Those—" Nimziki cut himself off when the president walked into the room. Whitmore looked at the paper map taped to the wall. The destroyed cities were marked with a black X. There were Xs all over the map.

"Atlanta, Chicago, and Philadelphia are confirmed destroyed, sir," said General Grey. "The ships are now reportedly heading for Miami, Fort Worth, and Memphis. They're definitely not wasting any time." He shot an accusatory glare at Nimziki. "They've obviously been planning this for a long time."

The president wanted to throw Nimziki through a wall, but there was no time for anger right now. He would deal with him in the future, if there was one.

"What about our forces, what do we have left?" the president asked.

"We're down to fifteen percent, sir," said General Grey. "If we calculate the time it's taking them to destroy a city and move on, we're looking at worldwide destruction of every major city within the next thirty-six hours."

Whitmore sat down for a moment to let this sink in. "We're being exterminated," he said.

Major Mitchell led Steve into the room. "Mr. President, I have the pilot you wanted to meet."

Steve was still wearing the same dirty, sweat-soaked flight suit. He really didn't feel like meeting the president, but it wasn't really up to him, anyway.

"Captain Steven Hiller, sir," Steve saluted.

"At ease, Captain," said the president. "It's an honor to meet you. You did an incredible job out there today."

"Thank you, sir. Just doing my job, sir," said Steve.

"Where is the prisoner now?" asked Whitmore.

"We have it in isolation," said Major Mitchell. "The doctors are very hopeful that it will survive."

"I'd like to see it," said the president.

"Yes, sir," said Mitchell, and showed him out of the room.

Steve walked over to General Grey and introduced himself. "General," he said, "I'm really anxious to get back to El Toro, if it's all right."

The general couldn't think of any easy way to break the news to him. "Didn't anyone tell you? El Toro's been taken out. Destroyed. I'm sorry."

Steve stood there frozen as the general walked away.

———

"OKAY, GUYS, DINNER IS SERVED," SAID
Jasmine. She had collected an assortment of canned
foods from the ruined cafeteria and headed back to
the broken-down hangar where they had set up
camp. Some of the injured men had started a little
fire near Mrs. Whitmore and had tried to make her a
bed out of cardboard and folded clothes. When she
saw Jasmine coming, the First Lady tried to sit up a
little. The movement obviously caused her a great
deal of pain.

"Hey, hey, don't move, okay? Try to keep as still as
you can," Jasmine said.

The two women stared into the fire for a long time
without saying anything. Dylan was scooping out a
can of baked beans and munching them down. He
was so happy to have food, he was dancing around
while he ate. Jasmine felt panicked as she watched
her little son. *Where will I get food tomorrow?* she
wondered.

"Your son," said Mrs. Whitmore weakly, "he's
beautiful."

"He's my angel," she said.

"Was his father stationed here?"

"He wasn't his father," said Jasmine, staring into
the fire. "I was kind of hoping he wanted the job,
though."

"Mommy, can I have some more food?" Dylan
asked as he came running over.

"Dylan, come here." She pulled him down into her

lap. "I want you to meet the First Lady." Dylan extended his hand to shake like a grown-up.

Mrs. Whitmore smiled. "That's funny, I thought you didn't recognize me."

"I didn't want to say anything," Jasmine said, and smiled apologetically. "I voted for the other guy."

THE NEW ALIEN SPECIMEN WAS STRAPPED TO an operating table in the operating room. A few of the smaller tentacles were still occasionally squirming, but the beast still appeared to be out cold. Dr. Okun and his three assistants prepared to investigate.

"Are the life-support monitors recording?" asked Okun.

"Yes," answered one of the assistants. "If we screw up, it will all be on tape."

"Okay," Okun started, "we're going to split the creature's skull down the middle and peel it back to reach the living creature inside. This," he slapped the outside skeleton, "is just a suit, like armor."

Okun inserted his chisel into the seam that ran down the center of the beast's face. He began to wriggle it back and forth. It was like trying to pry open the world's largest clam. It finally flew open with a sudden *thwack*. Everyone, including Okun, jumped back.

"Oh, my God," said Okun and turned his head away, "that smell is so awful."

"They conquered space travel, but not BO," an assistant added.

Okun returned to the table with a small pair of surgical scissors. "And now for the really icky part." He began to cut into the folds of oozing white tissue that hid the little creature inside. It looked like a caterpillar hibernating in a deep cocoon. It didn't seem possible that anything could live inside. Okun pulled back the layers and revealed the creature within. It looked exactly like the ones floating in the tubes behind them, only its skin was more purple.

"Okay, let's pull it out of there. I'll—" Okun suddenly fell backward into the surgical trays and gripped his head in pain.

"Doctor? Doctor, are you all right?"

Dr. Okun was now staring blankly into space.

"Doctor, the alien's arm is moving. Should I increase the sodium pentothal? Doctor?"

There was no answer from the doctor. Suddenly the alien snapped the restraints and raised up on its haunches. Its tentacles were flailing everywhere, knocking over instruments and breaking lights. A vacuum tube tore loose and began to blow great quantities of steam into the air. Each of the assistants jumped as far back as they could get, but it was difficult to see anything in the dark, steamy room. One grabbed a scalpel. One ran for the door. It was jammed shut. The alien slapped and thrashed at the assistants using its arms and lightning-fast tentacles. They were no match for its amazing strength.

The vault-like door to the outer observation room opened and in stepped President Whitmore with Major Mitchell and General Grey. Behind the glass window was the operating room. It was dark and full of smoke. Obviously, something was wrong.

"Dr. Okun," Major Mitchell called. "Dr. Okun, can you hear me?"

There was no sound except for spewing steam and then—*slam!* Dr. Okun's blood-smeared body was thrown against the glass. It was difficult to tell whether or not he was alive. There was a long tentacle wrapped around his neck. Okun's mouth opened and words came out, but the voice was not his.

"Release me, will kill," said the gravelly voice.

"We've got to get him out of there," said Major Mitchell. He started toward the door.

"Stay where you are," ordered General Grey. "Dr. Okun, can you hear me?"

"Release me," the voice repeated, "now."

It was clear that the alien was speaking through the doctor. He was controlling his body like a ventriloquist. The steam in the room was beginning to clear and the men could now see what was holding Okun against the glass. The creature was hanging half out of its suit and began to approach the window. Once more it punched at the window with Okun's limp body.

Whitmore stepped up to the glass and addressed the alien. "Why have you come here? What do your people want?"

The gravelly voice came from Okun's body again. "Air, water, food, your sun."

"Where is your home?"

"Here, now," said the voice.

"And before here, where did you come from?" Whitmore asked.

"Many worlds."

"We have plenty of resources to share," the president said carefully. "Perhaps, we could live together in peace."

"Peace?" said the voice. "No peace."

"What is it that you want us to do?"

The alien didn't answer through Dr. Okun this time. He sent a telepathic message to Whitmore. Suddenly, the president jolted backward and grabbed his head. The alien had sent him a glimpse of what they had done to other planets and what they had in store for earth. The president quickly saw that these creatures would have no mercy. To the aliens, humans were filthy little rats that needed to be exterminated. They planned to kill all the people on the planet.

"Is that glass bulletproof?" Grey asked Mitchell.

"No, sir," he said. With that, they both pulled out their weapons and took aim at the creature inside. They fired three times each. The alien was stunned by the bullets and quickly came crashing down. Okun collapsed on the ground. He was dead. The president lay motionless on the floor.

"Mr. President, are you all right?" Grey asked.

The president began to speak. He had a look of horror and disgust on his face. "It wanted me to understand. It communicated with me. They're like parasites. They travel from planet to planet and use up everything. When they've ruined the place, they move on." He stood up and brushed himself off. He was a little bit dazed by the whole experience, but he was clear on the words he was about to speak.

"General Grey, coordinate a missile strike. I want a nuclear warhead sent to every one of their ships. Immediately."

STEVE HAD WALKED BACK OUT TO WHERE the former caravan was still sitting. Everyone he walked by wanted to know about the alien and what was going on inside. They also wanted to know why they weren't allowed in. Steve smiled and tried to answer their questions, but his mind was not with them. He had spied a couple of transport helicopters sitting in a nearby hangar and was making his way toward them. He was trying to act like he was on official business until he got close enough to jump inside. He quickly started the engine and was about to lift off when a soldier shouted.

"What do you think you're doing? Get out of

there!" The man speaking was the size of two Steves put together.

"I'm just going to borrow this. I'll be right back," Steve yelled over the engine noise.

"No, you're not, sir." And with that he pointed his gun at Steve.

"Do you really want to shoot me?" Steve stared at him.

The soldier clearly didn't know what to do. "Oh, man! I'm gonna catch hell for this!"

Steve began to lift off. "Just tell them I hit you," he yelled.

The large man just stared at Steve. That would be like telling his boss that a fly had bitten him.

DAVID SAT IN A SMALL LUNCH ROOM IN AREA 51 and fixed himself another drink. He had found some scotch hidden in the back of a cupboard and was determined to finish the bottle. So far, he was making good progress. Connie walked in and watched him down a gulp. She knew he didn't normally drink, so he must know about the president's decision to launch nuclear warheads.

"I take it you've heard," she said.

"A toast," David held up another glass, "to the end of the world."

"He didn't come to this decision lightly, you know. He's a good man, David."

David stared into his glass and laughed. "He'd better be. You left me for him."

She started to get upset.

"Sorry, sorry," David said, "for your career."

Connie was hurt by his words. "It wasn't just my career, David. It was the single most important chance of my life. I wanted my life to have meaning. I wanted to make a difference." She looked up at him as he poured himself another one. "Haven't you ever wanted to be part of something special?"

David slammed down the bottle. "I was part of something special."

She had hurt him, she knew. She started to leave the room and stopped at the door. "If it makes any difference, I never stopped loving you."

"But that wasn't enough, right?" he asked.

With tears in her eyes, she left without answering.

GENERAL GREY HAD PUT TOGETHER A nuclear strike. Some radio and radar capabilities had been restored, so he was able to contact the surrounding air force bases and quickly get some B-52 bombers in the air. They flew off toward the city destroyers around the country.

"Which target will we reach first?" asked the president as he entered the Area 51's command center.

"Houston, Texas, sir. We should reach our target in six minutes."

"My God, Houston," said the president. What he was about to do was beginning to sink in.

"The city has been evacuated sir," General Grey said. "Civilian casualties should be at a minimum."

All eyes then turned to the computer tracking map on the wall. They were watching the plane approach its target. Whitmore asked for a moment of silence. He whispered a prayer to himself, and then said to the room, "May our children forgive us."

The B–52 launched its nuclear missile at the city destroyer above Houston. The room was tense and silent except for Nimziki, who shouted with glee when they saw the bomb explode on the screen.

"It's a hit!" he yelled.

A giant mushroom cloud began to form over the spot where Houston used to be. It was now gone. Whitmore and his staff watched the fuzzy glow on the screen and waited to see if it had worked. Then the report came in from the pilot.

"Target remains intact, sir," he said. "It's confirmed, the target is in good shape and moving in over Houston."

"Call the other planes back," Whitmore said softly.

Nimziki couldn't believe they were giving up so easily. "The other bombers might have better luck. You can't just give up—"

"I said call them back," the president commanded.

Whitmore slumped into a chair. He felt completely beaten. He didn't know what else to do.

JASMINE SAT STARING INTO THE LAST
flames of the dying fire. Mrs. Whitmore was trying to
rest, but Jasmine could see that she was in a lot of
pain. Dylan and Boomer were curled up together at
her feet. In the distance she could hear the beating of
helicopter blades. She saw a huge spotlight and
thought maybe the White House had sent someone to
look for Mrs. Whitmore.

After flying overhead, the helicopter landed right
beside the bombed-out hangar. Jasmine got up to greet
the pilot. Out jumped Steve. Jasmine smiled the
biggest smile ever and jumped into his arms.

"You're late!" she said.

Steve pulled her back a moment to get a good look
at the girl he loved.

"Well, you know how I like to make a big entrance!"
He pulled her close to him and they kissed.

STEVE AND JASMINE QUICKLY GOT MRS.
Whitmore to the medical facility at Area 51. Dr.
Isaacs had the president alerted that his wife had
arrived.

"How is she?" asked the president as he rushed by
the doctor with Patricia in his arms. He set Patty down
and she ran into the room where her mother was
resting.

"Be very gentle, okay, Patricia?" Dr. Isaacs called behind her. "Your mommy is very sick."

But Patricia was gone. She burst into the room. "Mommy!" She rushed over and laid her head on Mrs. Whitmore's arm. "We were worried. We didn't know where you were."

"I'm here now, honey." Mrs. Whitmore was in a lot of pain, but she was trying not to show it.

Dr. Isaacs stopped the president before he walked into the room. "I'm sorry, Mr. President. If we had gotten to her sooner, maybe there would have been something we could've done. . . ."

"What? Wait, what are you saying?" he asked.

"I'm sorry, sir, she's bleeding internally, and there's nothing else we can do," Dr. Isaacs said.

President Whitmore stood there for a moment. He wanted to scream and pound a wall with his fists. He walked into the room where his wife and daughter were talking.

"Why don't we let Mommy get some rest, munchkin?" he said to Patty.

"Okay." Patty kissed her mom's cheek. Connie came into the room and took Patty by the hand.

Marilyn didn't have to pretend for her husband. "I'm so scared, Tom," she said through tears.

"Hey, none of that," he said. "The doctor says you're going to be fine."

President Whitmore couldn't keep the truth from his wife. She could see the sorrow in his eyes.

"Liar," she said and smiled at him tenderly.

The two of them put their heads together and cried. They kissed and looked into each other's eyes until Marilyn fell asleep for the last time.

DAVID WAS WAY PAST DRUNK BY NOW. HE was miserable. He was knocking everything over that he touched and falling all over the place. Julius found him throwing trash around the room.

"David! What are you doing?"

"I'm making a mess! We've got to ruin the planet, Pops! We should burn the rain forest and dump all of our toxic waste. Maybe if we screw up our planet bad enough, they won't want it anymore."

David swung his leg to kick a can and landed on his butt. Julius walked over to help him up.

"Come on, son, I think you'd better sleep it off," Julius said. "Now get off that floor before you catch a cold. You know your mother used to always say—"

David cut him off. "Wait, wait, what'd you just say?"

"I said sleep, I said floor, I said cold. What else did I say?" Julius asked.

"Pops, you're a genius!" David kissed his father's cheek and ran out of the room.

A FEW HOURS LATER DAVID HAD SOBERED up and convinced Connie to bring everyone down to the hangar where the alien attacker ship was housed.

"All right, Connie, we're here," said Nimziki. "What's this all about?"

"I really have no idea. David just asked me to get everyone here," she said.

Dylan was sitting on Steve's shoulders when they walked in. Dylan couldn't believe his eyes. The ship was just like the ones in cartoons. "Hey, can that thing fly in outer space?"

"It sure can, bub," Steve said.

David came out of the attacker cockpit and greeted the room full of people. He set a soda can on the tip of the wing and faced the onlookers.

"Major Mitchell, do you think you can shoot this can off the ship?" Mitchell looked to the president to see if he should try. The president nodded his approval and Mitchell took out his gun and fired. The bullet hit the shield and bounced around the room. Everyone screamed and ducked.

"Sorry, sorry, my fault," said David. "You see, the reason you couldn't hit the ship is because of its protective shield."

"We know that already. What's your point?" Nimziki asked.

"My point is," David said as he sat down on the wing and quickly typed into his laptop, "if we can't beat their defenses, then we have to get around them. Major Mitchell, when you're ready."

Major Mitchell was not too thrilled about firing again. The president gave him the go ahead. He fired and knocked the can across the room.

"How did you do that?" General Grey asked.

"I gave it a cold," said David.

Everyone was staring at David in amazement. They had no idea what he meant by that, but they were all very impressed.

"More accurately, I gave it a virus, a computer virus," David explained.

General Grey didn't quite understand. He didn't trust computers, or people who were good with them. "Are you saying you can send out a signal that will bring down their shields?"

"Well, yes, but it's not that simple," said David as he walked over to the chart that he'd drawn. "The only way to infect them all would be to plant the virus into the signal coming from the mother ship. The infected signal would then be sent down to all of the city destroyers and attacker ships."

Nimziki found this whole plan humorous. "And just how do you propose we infect the mother ship with the virus?"

"Well," David started, "we'll have to fly this attacker ship out of our atmosphere and dock with the mother ship. Then we'll uhhh . . . " He could hear his own words and knew how crazy all of this sounded, but since no one else had a plan left, he figured he might as well tell them the whole thing. "We'll upload the virus and then get the heck out of there. We'll fly back down to earth."

"This is ridiculous," said Nimziki.

"How long could the shields be down?" Grey asked David.

"Well, uhh, it's hard to say for sure. It could be as long as two to three minutes before they discover it."

"So, let me get this straight," Nimziki started. "Are you suggesting that we coordinate a worldwide counterstrike with a window of only a few minutes?"

"With their shields down, it might be possible," Grey said.

"Please! You're not buying into any of this, are you?" Nimziki looked at the president. "We don't have the manpower or the resources to launch that kind of an attack. Not to mention that this whole cockeyed plan is dependent on flying a machine that no one in this world is qualified to operate."

Steve cleared his throat and stepped forward. "Excuse me. I think I could fly it, sir. I've seen these things in action, and I'm quite aware of their capabilities." He turned to the president. "With your permission, sir, I'd like to try."

Nimziki was ready to blow. He couldn't believe they had given up on the nuclear attack so easily and were now going to try something this stupid. He pointed at the alien attacker and said in a low voice, "That thing is a wreck. It crash-landed in the fifties. We don't even know if it's capable of flying."

This was David's cue. "All right!" he yelled to the technicians. "Remove the clamps!" Within moments, the massive forty-foot ship was hovering perfectly still about fifteen feet from the ground. David turned back to his amazed audience.

"Any other questions?"

President Whitmore turned to General Grey. "Let's do it."

Everyone began to move quickly. There were lots of plans to be made in a hurry.

David walked over to Steve. "Do you really think you can fly that thing?"

Steve shot back, "Do you really think you can do all of that bull you just fed us?"

The two smiled at each other. They knew they were in for a rocky ride.

WITHIN MINUTES, CONNIE, GENERAL GREY, and the president were planning the worldwide strike. The biggest immediate challenge would be getting the word out. As they hurried through the hallway, Secretary Nimziki caught up with them.

"I understand that you're upset over the death of your wife, but that's no excuse for making another huge mistake," he said nastily.

That was the last straw. President Whitmore grabbed Nimziki by the lapels and pushed him against a wall.

"The only mistake I ever made was appointing a sniveling little weasel like you secretary of defense. But that's one mistake, I'm happy to say, that I don't have to live with. Mr. Nimziki, you're fired."

Whitmore stepped back and almost smiled. "General Grey, organize every plane you can find and get me some pilots to fly them."

General Grey was proud of his boss. "Yes, sir."

Whitmore and Grey walked out of the room. Connie had to enjoy the moment for just a little while longer. Nimziki was in shock. He stood there brushing off his suit and shaking his head.

"He can't do that," he said to Connie.

"Well," she said smiling, "he just did!"

MILITARY TROOPS ALL OVER THE WORLD HAD run into the same frustrations that the Americans had. Nothing seemed to work against this enemy. Many had retreated into the deserts to hide out. They figured if they couldn't do battle with the aliens, they should at least get away from the city destroyers.

In the middle of the Saudi desert, a group of British, Arabs, Israelis, and Iraqis were trying to coexist. At least a hundred planes from all different countries were sitting out there in the middle of nowhere in the Saudi desert. An Arab man rushed into the British tent and announced that they were receiving some sort of a signal in Morse code. He wanted the men to come check it out and see if it was in English.

One of the British officers was quick to identify it. "It's from the Americans. They want to organize a counteroffensive."

The same message was being relayed all over the world. So many of Russia's pilots had been knocked out of the air, they had been sitting tight for hours just waiting for someone to have an idea. The same was true in Korea, Japan, Germany, France, England, Italy, and Spain.

Everyone heard the whole plan laid out over the wire in Morse code. On any other day, most of these countries would be shooting at one another, but today they could work together against their new common enemy.

"HOW ARE WE DOING?" PRESIDENT Whitmore asked General Grey.

"Better than expected," he reported. Grey showed Whitmore a combat-ready map that marked every spot in the world where planes were ready for battle. "Europe has been hit almost as hard as we have, but the Middle East and Asia still have fifty percent of their capabilities."

"And our troops here?" asked the president.

"Major Mitchell has plenty of planes stored on the

base, but we haven't got enough pilots to fly them," Grey said.

"Then find them," Whitmore ordered.

MIGUEL STEPPED INTO THE CASSE MOTOR home as quietly as he could. Troy was sleeping and Russell was at his side.

"How's he doing?" Miguel asked.

"He's just fine," said Russell.

"Russell, I just wanted to say, I'm sorry for what I said to you back there. I had no right."

"Oh, that's all right, Miguel." Russell walked over to the cabinet and pulled out a new bottle of whiskey. "Wanna join me in a little celebration?"

Miguel had been so proud of his father a few hours ago that he had convinced himself that Russell was changing. He looked at him now through the same sad, angry eyes. Miguel ran out of the motor home.

Russell walked out to look, but he was gone. Major Mitchell had pulled up with a bullhorn to the refugee camp of motor homes. He was asking for anyone with flight experience to please step forward. Russell spoke up.

"I'm a pilot. I can fly."

Mitchell looked at the sloppy man and then down at the bottle of booze in his hand. "Sorry, sir."

"No, wait, I can fly. You want people who can fly, I can fly."

Mitchell was ignoring him now.

"You don't understand!" Russell yelled after him. "These guys, they ruined my life."

Mitchell was already gone with a few new volunteers. Russell smashed his bottle onto the pavement.

GENERAL GREY BEGAN BRIEFING DAVID AND Steve on the adjustments that had been made to their attacker ship. Connie listened in, standing nearby in the hangar. He showed them how the nuclear missile they were going to unload had been hidden on the plane. He then showed Steve how to launch it. He held up a small black box.

"This will be attached to the ship's main console," General Grey said.

"It's just like an AMRAAM launch pad on a stealth," said Steve.

"Exactly, use it the same way," said General Grey. "There's only one difference. We've programmed the nuke so it won't explode on impact. When you launch it, you'll have thirty seconds to get away."

It was a comfort to David to hear that Steven Hiller did actually sound like he knew what he was doing. But thirty seconds didn't sound to David like enough time to go anywhere.

"Aagghh!" said Steve as he looked at his watch. "We're late!" He ran out of the storage hangar.

"We'll be right there," David called after him.

"Thirty seconds," Connie said to David, "don't you think that's cutting it a bit close?"

David didn't want Connie to know he had been thinking the same thing. "Oh, honey, we'll be far away from there by the time that thing explodes."

A technician was busy attaching a transmitter to the bottom of the ship.

"It's the strongest one we could get," he said to David. "It'll tell us when you've uploaded the virus."

"Then cross your fingers that the shields go down," David said.

Constance was alarmed to hear that even the shields were not a sure thing. "Why you?" she called after him. "Why can't you show someone else how to plant this virus? Someone more trained for this mission?"

"Who would that be?" asked David, grinning. He liked the fact that she was worrying about him. "What if some last-minute adjustment needs to be made?"

David walked over to the recycling bin and picked up a can off the countertop. "You know how I'm always trying to save the planet?" He tossed the can in the bin. "Well, here's my chance." David went back to grab his laptop.

"*Now* he gets ambitious," Connie said to herself.

"DYLAN, ZIP ME UP." JASMINE SUCKED IN her breath as Dylan yanked on the dress' zipper.

"It's too tight," he complained.

"Well, I had to borrow it." Jasmine stood up and faced her son for approval. "How do I look?"

Dylan gave her the so-so hand wave.

"Oh, thanks, you're a lot of help!" she said.

She was ready. Now it was just up to Steve to show up. Finally, thought Jasmine, they were getting married. It only took an alien invasion to get him to ask. But that was all right with her. All she could think about now was getting him back after this crazy mission to the mother ship.

"Sorry I'm late, Jas," Steve said as he rushed in. He looked her over in the tight dress. "Wow, you look amazing. Wow."

She punched him playfully in the arm. "Well, now that you've made your big entrance, let's get this goin'."

"First, Jas, I want to apologize," Steve said.

"For what?" she asked.

"I should have done this a long time ago," he said.

The base chaplain was ready to get the show on the road. "Are you ready?" he asked.

"Yes," they both said. Dylan followed them to the front of the room.

"Witnesses?" asked the chaplain.

Just as he asked the question, David and Constance came through the door. They quickly took their seats on either side of the aisle.

"Steve, do you have the ring?" the chaplain asked.

"Oh, yeah." Steve reached into his pocket and pulled out the dolphin ring that Jimmy had caught him with the day before.

The short ceremony was special for David and Connie, too. Connie saw that David was still wearing his wedding ring. She reached across the aisle and held his hand.

OUTSIDE OF AREA 51, THE AIRFIELD WAS full of busy technicians, chattering pilots, and plenty of planes. The caravan of refugees mingled amid the crowd. There was a nervous excitement in the air. The world's last attempt to beat the aliens was about to take place.

The president walked out to join all of the activity with General Grey at his side.

"They look a little nervous," he said to Grey as he surveyed the volunteers. It was a wide mix of people, from military pilots to bikers to salesmen to doctors. Young and old, fat and thin. Whoever knew how to fly a plane was there. Whitmore decided it was time to address them. He stepped up into the back of the truck and grabbed Mitchell's PA system.

"Good morning." Everyone quickly gathered around to listen to their president. Whitmore took a long pause to think about the words that these people could carry with them into the battle.

"In less than an hour, planes from here and all over the world will be launching the largest aerial battle in the history of mankind." He paused to think about that idea.

"Mankind. The word has new meaning for all of us now. We are reminded not of our petty differences but of our common interests. Perhaps it's fate that today is the Fourth of July, and we will once again be fighting for our freedom. Not from tyranny or oppression, but from annihilation. We're fighting for our right to live, to exist."

"From this day on, the Fourth of July will no longer be remembered as an American holiday, but as the day that the world declared in one voice that we will not go quietly into the night. We will not vanish without a fight. We're going to live on. We're going to survive. Today, we celebrate our Independence Day!"

The crowd erupted into applause and cheers. President Whitmore walked through the crowd and shook hands. Major Mitchell showed him over to the table where his flight suit and choice of helmets were waiting. General Grey finally caught up to him.

"Mr. President, I'd sure like to know what you're doing."

"I'm a pilot, Will." He smiled at his old friend. "I belong in the air."

Grey didn't like what he was hearing, but he understood why the president had made this choice.

IN THE LAST FEW MINUTES BEFORE TAKE-OFF, the research staff had checked and rechecked the attacker ship's equipment. There were scraps of paper with instructions scribbled on them taped all over the dashboard.

It was tough for everyone to say their good-byes to David and Steve. They had a million chances to fail and only one to succeed.

"When I'm back, we'll light the rest of those fireworks," Steve told Dylan. Jasmine gave Steve a long hug and kiss and watched him walk toward the ship. She was afraid it would be the last time she ever saw him.

"I'm very proud of you, son," Julius said to David. David had never heard these words come out of his father's mouth. He smiled. "Here, take these." Julius had swiped a few barf bags from Air Force One and thought that now would be a good time to get some use out of them. "Just in case," he added.

"Thanks, Pops. Oh, I've got something here for you, too." He reached into his computer case and handed his father his yarmulke and a leather-bound Bible. Julius was amazed. This was the last thing he ever expected to receive. "Just in case," David said.

Connie couldn't believe David was leaving. After years of fighting and pain, she had finally felt like they were connecting again. And now he was leaving. It was hard for her not to cry. "Be careful," was all she could say.

"Wait! Wait! We can't go yet!" Steve shouted. "Does anyone have any cigars?"

Julius produced two from his pocket. "My last two, with my blessings."

"Thanks, you're a life saver," Steve said to Julius. "I almost just jinxed the whole thing."

Steve handed one of the cigars to David. "Here's our Victory Dance cigars. Very important. But you can't light up till the fat lady sings."

A few seconds later, Steve was heading up the ladder. David gave one last nervous smile around the hangar. Then he climbed inside.

CONNIE JOINED JASMINE AND THE OTHERS in the observation booth. They watched as the enormous hangar doors opened mechanically.

David and Steve strapped themselves in and took another look at the instrument panel in front of them. Steve noticed the little bags sitting on David's lap.

"What are those for?"

"Oh, I'm, uhh, not real big on flying," David confessed.

"Great," said Steve, "just aim that way." He pointed to the other side of the cockpit.

Outside, the clamps on the attacker were removed

and the ship floated steadily about twelve feet off the ground. Steve was excited beyond words.

"Are you ready? Let's rock 'n' roll!"

David felt sick even before the ship started moving.

Steve jerked it forward then backward. "Oops, let's try that again." He threw the gear around once more and the ship started sailing forward. It quickly sped out of the hangar. Before anyone could get too upset or excited, they were gone.

They were blasting full speed ahead, straight for the mother ship which was now hovering just outside earth's atmosphere. The attacker was bobbing, wobbling, and performing an occasional loop along the way. David was feeling every move like he was taking a nosedive off Niagara Falls.

"Steve, what are you doing? Don't do that, please," David said.

Steve was having the time of his life. "I have *got* to get me one of these! Whoo-hoo!"

THE PRESIDENT HAD SEEN THE ATTACKER take off from the cockpit of his plane. It shot by so quickly it looked like a black streak in the sky. Whitmore strapped on his helmet and spoke with Area 51's command center.

"Grey, do you read me?"

"Roger, Eagle One, loud and clear. Stand by, sir." Whitmore could hear in Grey's voice that something was wrong. "Our primary target has shifted course. Looks like our secret is out. They're headed right for us, sir. Estimated time of arrival is thirty-six minutes."

President Whitmore had hoped for some practice time with his thrown-together fleet, but now that was out of the question.

DAVID LAID BACK IN HIS SEAT LIKE A crumpled candy wrapper. He moaned and groaned with his eyes closed. Steve finally took pity on his woozy copilot and straightened the ship out. They watched out the window as the blue sky evaporated. The next moment, they were surrounded by stars as far as they could see in every direction. For Steve, his lifelong dream was fulfilled at last.

"I've waited a long time for this," he said.

A few minutes later, they began to get their first glimpses of the monstrous mother ship. The sight was horrifying but intriguing. David began to snap out of his queasiness.

"That's it," he said to Steve. "Head straight for it."

"Wait a minute, something's happening," said Steve. "I can't move the controls."

"I had a feeling this would happen. They're bringing us in," David said.

"You had a feeling? When were you planning on telling me about this feeling?" asked Steve.

"Oops." David smiled.

LONG BEFORE THE CITY DESTROYER WAS
within range of Area 51, its hulking fifteen-mile-wide
frame could be seen cruising above the horizon. The
president kept his squadron positioned well above the
approaching ship and in attack formation. "We have
visual," Whitmore reported back to base.

"Do not engage until we have confirmation that the
package has been delivered," General Grey
commanded.

"Roger," said the president.

Connie sat down in front of Major Mitchell to ask
him a question that had been bothering her for a while
now. "What if that thing, the ship, gets here before
David has a chance to plant that virus?"

"We're pretty deep underground here. It should
give us some protection," he answered. He really
didn't have time to deal with her questions.

"What about the people outside?"

Mitchell had never even thought about the refugees
outside. He was used to thinking about strategies,
secrets, even aliens, but not people. He stood up and
dashed out of the room with Connie.

THE MOTHER SHIP WAS THE SIZE OF A SMALL
planet sliced cleanly in half. The underside looked
like a giant seed pod. In row after row, there were the

domes of the massive city destroyers. There seemed to be an endless number of the fifteen-mile-wide ships spanning across the five-hundred-mile-wide mother ship. Thirty-six empty rings showed where the giant city destroyers had once been docked. Hanging off two sides of the craft were a pair of fang-like structures. Each one was at least one hundred miles tall. The mother ship had looked like a helmet in satellite photos. Now it looked like a cobra to the men.

Steve and David's ship was moving so quickly through the entrance tunnel to the mother ship, they could hardly see all of the intricate details on the walls and ceilings. Once inside, they noticed hundreds of attacker ships just like theirs. They looked like dots compared to the mother ship.

The tunnel they were traveling through finally ended. They were now in the central chamber of the mother ship, and for several moments neither of them could see a thing. Everything looked like soupy blue fog. As soon as their eyes adjusted, they were treated to a horrifying sight. Aliens. Thousands of them. They were working on and around hundreds of attacker ships.

"Looks like they're preparing for an invasion," Steve said.

Their attacker was lifted higher and then grabbed from the top by a set of huge prongs.

"This isn't gonna work," Steve said. "They're going to see us before we can do anything."

"Not to worry," David said as he flipped some

switches, "this ship comes fully loaded. It's got reclining bucket seats, an AM/FM radio and . . . power windows." As he flipped the final switch, a black screen came up over their windows.

Once the clamps outside were fully connected to their ship, a data exchange began. Now, David could begin his work. He began to type information into his laptop at a frantic pace. Changes in the ship's signal began to flash across the screen. The words "Negotiating with Host" appeared on his laptop. He held his breath as the signal analyzer program sorted through the billions of possibilities. Then, much sooner than he had expected, the machine beeped and displayed a new message. It was a miracle. It read, "Connecting to Host."

"We're in! I can't believe it! We're in!" David cheered.

"Great. Now let's get out." Steve was less than thrilled to be trapped in there much longer.

"Okay, I'm uploading the virus," said David.

"HE'S UPLOADING THE VIRUS," A technician reported at Area 51's command center.

Grey stopped frowning for a split second. He picked up a handheld microphone and sent his voice into the sky. "Eagle One, do you read?"

"Affirmative," Whitmore answered, "loud and clear."

"The package is being delivered," said Grey. "Stand by to engage."

"Roger."

ABOVEGROUND AT AREA 51, THERE WAS NO such excitement. The movement of the refugees into the hangar had begun in an orderly fashion, but as soon as the destroyer could be seen on the horizon, that changed. Panic swept over the airfield. People were screaming and running toward the hangar doors.

Alicia had already sent Troy inside, and now she was rummaging through the few things that she had in the motor home, trying to decide what to keep. Philip helped her gather up a few things.

"We better get inside and find your brothers," he said.

"You're right," said Alicia.

All around them panicked people ran in every direction. The two held hands and tried to pretend everything was okay. It almost worked until Miguel ran up behind them.

"Have you guys seen Russell? I've looked everywhere."

Neither had seen Russell for quite a while.

"COME ON, COME ON," DAVID SAID. THEY couldn't wait much longer for this virus to upload. And then, it happened. "Upload Complete" the laptop read.

Back at Area 51's command center, the message came through.

"Unbelievable," was all General Grey could say. He got on the radio to let Whitmore and his men know that the time was now.

"Eagle One, this is base. The delivery is complete. Engage."

"With pleasure, Base," Whitmore said.

Whitmore gave the signal to the others to accelerate. They followed his lead for a swift bombing run on the city destroyer. The president's bay door split open and the first AMRAAM missile computed its flight and locked on its target.

"Come on, baby," Whitmore said.

A quarter of a mile from the surface of the destroyer, the AMRAAM exploded harmlessly. The shields were still in place.

"That's it," said General Grey. "Eagle One, disengage. I want you out of there immediately."

"Negative!" shouted the president. "Everybody, maintain your formation." The president allowed another AMRAAM to drop out of his plane. The planes were so close to the invisible shield by now that they had to turn back. As they did, they all heard the explosion. The second bomb had hit. It made a huge gash in the side of the destroyer, the size of a football field.

The Area 51 command center erupted into cheers. Even General Grey hugged a technician.

"We're going back in," Whitmore announced. "Squad leaders, take point." The top pilots spread themselves out for the others to follow. One by one, each pilot dropped their missiles, but many of the pilots lacked the military know-how, and their missiles didn't make it. About thirty of the missiles did connect, though, and the city destroyer was damaged in many places.

Then, the moment they all feared arrived. The door to the city destroyer opened and a swarm of attacker ships flew out. They spread out in all directions to take on the earthlings. An aerial dogfight was in full swing.

Several of the attackers left the rest of the pack and headed for Area 51.

MIGUEL WAS STILL ON THE AIRFIELD looking for Russell and he was running out of time. He turned to look at the massive battle going on above. He heard the boom of the missiles connecting. *Maybe we can win after all,* he thought. His search for his dad came to a quick end when he saw the attackers headed his way. He took off running as fast as he could go. Laser fire was hitting all around him. Motor homes were exploding and flipping off the ground. The last of the refugees who hadn't made it inside were running in terror. Across the field in the hangar, Miguel could see a soldier and a woman waving people inside. He decided to make a run for it. The pulsing laser fire ripped into the ground all around him. He raced through the steel doors just as the soldier was rolling them closed. Miguel followed the woman to the elevator. A loud blast rocked the huge steel structure and blew the hangar doors completely off.

Connie pushed Miguel and the few others into the elevator and pushed the button. Just as the doors closed, the entire top structure gave way and collapsed.

STEVE AND DAVID WERE MORE THAN READY to get out of the mother ship. But now that they were ready, they couldn't move their attacker. Steve was trying everything he knew. Nothing was working.

"Try something else!" David yelled.

"What does it look like I'm doin'? I can't shake her free," Steve yelled back. "These clamps are too strong."

David started to flip switches all over the dash. Nothing. He then started typing frantically into his laptop. Suddenly, the windowshade came down.

"What are you doing? They're gonna see us!" Steve shouted.

"It's not me. They're overriding the system," said David.

Both men hit the deck.

"Why don't you take a look?" David said.

"Be my guest," said Steve.

David still didn't move, so Steve finally gave in. He raised up just a little and quickly threw himself back down. Staring through the front shield were several aliens.

"There's a whole bunch of 'em looking in here," Steve said.

"Did they see you?" David asked.

"Sure. There's twenty or thirty of 'em looking this way! Yes, they saw me!"

"Then, Steve . . . why are we still hiding?"

David raised himself up slowly to see what Steve had seen. He sat back down in the chair.

"Check and mate," said David.

AS THE BLASTS FROM ABOVE CONTINUED TO rock Area 51's interior, the lights flashed on and off. Hundreds of the refugees stood shoulder to shoulder in the underground labs screaming, hugging, and crying.

Julius had gathered a group of frightened children. He sat them down in a circle and told them it was okay to be a little scared, but everything was going to be all right. "Let's all join hands," he said. He unfolded his yarmulke and set it on top of his head. He began to recite some verse from the Torah. Most of the kids didn't understand a word he was saying, but it did somehow make them feel better.

Julius saw Nimziki standing to one side, looking lost and frightened.

"Join us," he said to the former secretary of defense.

Nimziki sat down in the circle. "But I'm not Jewish."

"Nobody's perfect," said Julius.

Miguel entered the lab full of people and spotted Alicia with Philip. Alicia called to him, "Did you find Russell?"

"I'm still looking! Stay where you are. I'll be right back," said Miguel as he ran out of the room.

Philip put his arm around Alicia. *Just my luck,* she thought, *I find a nice guy on the last night on earth.*

THE CITY DESTROYER CONTINUED ON ITS path toward Area 51. Although the bombs had inflicted some damage to it, it wasn't stopping. Many of the inexperienced pilots had wasted their missiles.

"We're running out of firepower," a technician reported to Grey, "and we haven't caused much damage to the target."

President Whitmore's squad of thirty planes had been reduced to eight. Between all of them, they had fewer than ten missiles left.

Connie walked into the command center and stood behind General Grey. A technician rushed over to them to point out that the city destroyer was now directly overhead and its main door was beginning to open. The door that hid the large tower-like device that had blown the White House to bits.

"Attention!" General Grey said. "They're opening the big doors and getting ready to fire their gun. Somebody get down there and knock that thing out before they can use it!"

Miguel had slipped into the back of the room and was listening to all of the commotion.

"Roger, base," President Whitmore returned, "I've got one AMRAAM left and I'm on my way." He threw his plane into a steep turn. "You boys keep 'em off my tail." He fired his final missiles, but the timing was all wrong. Planes of every kind were darting back and forth through everyone's airspace. One got in the way of his missile and exploded.

"I'm out of missiles! Eagle Two, take point. I'll drop back and try to buy you some time."

"I'm on it," answered Eagle Two. Behind him, the other pilots were yelling out the positions of the incoming attackers. The attackers swirled about everywhere. They surrounded Eagle Two and blasted him out of the sky.

"Does anybody up here have any missiles left?" asked the president.

"Sorry I'm late, Mr. President," someone said over the radio.

The president spotted an old red biwing just below

him. The plane was sputtering through the air. He could see the pilot was wearing an old-fashioned leather helmet and goggles. Strapped to the side of the plane with a bunch of old rope was something that looked like a missile.

"Don't worry, sir," Russell pointed to the missile strapped to his plane, "I'm packin'." Russell had stolen the heaviest, nastiest missile he could find. "I just need you to keep those guys off of me for a few more seconds."

Whitmore could see a whole new swarm of attackers moving in. The American pilots moved in on them and laid out covering fire to protect the old biwing.

"Pilot, identify yourself," General Grey commanded.

"Name's Russell Casse. I want you to do me a favor . . . " Russell paused. He was headed straight for the center of the ship. "Tell my children I love them very much."

"Russell?" Miguel came rushing forward to the microphone.

"Miguel? Is that you? You probably don't understand, but this is just something I've got to do, son. You were always better at taking care of them than me anyway." He snapped off his radio and threw his plane into the steepest climb it could take.

"All right, you aliens! In the words of my generation, 'UP YOURS!'"

Russell plowed straight into the huge opening where the giant needle-like probe stuck out, waiting to fire on the people below.

Russell had waited ten long years for a moment as perfect as this one. He hadn't planned on sacrificing his life for revenge, but the chance was here, and he had to take it.

"HELLO BOYS!" he screamed. "I'M BAACK!"

The old plane plowed nose first into the side of the firing weapon, causing a tiny puff of an explosion. But just as the deadly beam began to fire from the destroyer, it quickly cut itself off. The huge ship lifted up and away with incredible speed and every attacker followed it. But in a matter of seconds the whole retreat ended.

Beginning at the center of the massive destroyer, an explosion burst a hole through the domed roof. The body of the ship then seemed to melt from within. Internal explosions went off one after the other. It became a giant plate of fire and fell in huge flaming chunks onto the desert below.

In the command center below, the room erupted into cheers. This time, though, the celebration lasted. Miguel looked at his feet. He didn't know how to feel.

General Grey approached one of the celebrating technicians. "Get back on the wire. Tell everyone around the world how to shoot these monsters down."

STEVE THOUGHT IT WAS OVER. "I THINK I hear the fat lady singing," he said to David, pulling out his cigar. "I guess there's nothing left to do except nuke 'em and call it a day."

David was still in a staring contest with the creatures behind the glass. But he also now believed there was no other alternative. They would have to die with the aliens in order to save the planet.

David lit up his cigar and looked at it. "Funny, I always thought things like this would kill me."

Steve got off the floor and into his pilot's chair. He opened the little black box and punched in the launch code. He turned to David and extended his hand. "Hey man, it's been a pleasure."

"Likewise," said David, "and we almost got away with it."

"Ready?" Steve asked.

Both of the men stood up and started waving like idiots. The aliens were truly puzzled.

"Bye-bye. Good-bye. Take care. Bye-bye." They waved and waved.

"Do you think they know what's coming?" Steve asked.

"Not a chance," said David as he continued to wave, "Bye-now."

As Steve's finger touched the button, the floor of the tiny cabin jerked backwards. Both men fell down and the eight-foot missile shot away in a shower of sparks. It shot through the control tower and lodged into a wall. With their atmosphere ruined, the aliens began to choke and die from the exposure to space.

As this gruesome show went on, the clamps unexpectedly let go of David and Steve's attacker.

"We're loose!" Steve shouted.

"Doesn't matter," said David, "look at the countdown."

22 . . . 21 . . . 20

"I don't hear no fat lady," said Steve, and kicked the ship into high gear. Five attackers began to follow close behind them, down the tunnel. Swerving and twisting, they shot through the maze of the mother ship's interior. The attackers were firing at them from all sides. Steve shot through the triangular passageway that led to the exit.

"It's closing!" yelled David. "The door is closing!"

"I can see that! Stop side-seat driving!" Steve yelled back at him. Steve roared on toward the closing porthole. He looked down at the black box.

09 . . . 08 . . . 07

The porthole was almost shut. Steve decided to go for it. David closed his eyes. With only inches to spare, they made it through.

Out in space, Steve located the earth and steered the ship toward it.

01 . . . 00.

The engines died and everything went quiet. For a moment, the craft glided along silently at several hundred thousand miles per hour. Then there was a flash of light so bright it felt as if they had touched the sun. The force of the blast caught them from behind and tumbled their ship like a boulder rolling downhill all the way back to earth.

THE PRESIDENT STEPPED OUT OF HIS PLANE and the crowd of people went wild. Everyone was cheering and hugging the heroic pilots as they stepped out of their planes. The president and his fellow pilots made their way down to the secured laboratory room where hundreds of refugees were still holding out. When they walked into the room, the crowd erupted into more cheers for the pilots who had saved their lives. Patricia charged down the walkway and jumped into her father's arms.

Miguel found Troy and Alicia in the waiting crowd. One look at his face told them that Russell was dead. The three stood and hugged silently in the middle of all the celebration.

AS PRESIDENT WHITMORE ENTERED THE command center, more cheers broke out. General Grey was relieved to see his commander-in-chief back on the ground.

"How's the rest of the attack going?—

"Excellent. We have eight confirmed knock-downs."

Connie and Jasmine walked into the room to hear the updates.

"And our delivery boys?" Whitmore asked. "Any word on them?"

"Unfortunately," answered Grey, "we lost contact with them about fifty minutes ago, a moment or two after the mother ship exploded." Whitmore stepped toward Connie to offer his condolences, but before he could say anything, one of the technicians shouted.

"Hold on! Something's coming in on radar!"

A MILITARY VEHICLE CRAMMED WITH PEOPLE sped across the desert. Major Mitchell was driving straight for a dark plume of smoke in front of them. Jasmine, Dylan, Connie, President Whitmore, Patricia, General Grey, and Julius made up the rest of the passengers. All were straining their eyes for any sign of anything.

In the distance they could now see a ruined attacker engulfed in flame. They could then see two small figures emerge from the wreckage. They were moving toward them. General Grey was ready to pull out his gun until he looked a little more closely. These were no aliens. They were smoking Victory Dance cigars.

Captain Steven Hiller and David Levinson had done the impossible and lived to tell about it.

Jasmine threw open the door as soon as the truck came to a halt and took off running across the desert.

She didn't stop until she was in her husband's arms. "You scared me to death!—

Steven lifted her into the air and twirled her around. "Yeah, but what an entrance!"

Connie wanted to jump into David's arms, too, but she held back just a little. He grabbed her as soon as she got close enough and gave her the biggest kiss of her life. "So," he asked shyly, "did it work?"

"Yes, yes," she said, laughing. "It worked beautifully."

Julius had to put in his two cents. He walked over to his son and pointed at the cigar. "So this is healthy?"

"No," David said, smiling around the cigar, "but I could get used to it."

President Whitmore congratulated Captain Hiller and shook David's hand.

"Not too bad, David, not too bad at all."

"Thank you, sir."

Patricia looked at her father and hugged him tightly. "Happy Fourth of July, Daddy."

"Happy Fourth, munchkin."

In the sky, chunks of the burning mother ship continued to fall. It looked like a magnificent fireworks display. Steve held Dylan on his shoulder and looked up at the sky.

"Didn't I promise you fireworks?" he asked.